In Perpetuity

HUGH A. FLOWERS

Paperback-Press
an imprint of A & S Publishing
A & S Holmes, Inc.

ISBN: 0692457313
ISBN-13: 978-0692457313

TABLE OF CONTENTS

.

ACKNOWLEDGMENTS

I'd like to give a special thank you to Nathalie Kelley for once again painting the perfect cover art for this book. You did a wonderful job.

My thanks also goes out to Tina Vyborny for her help. Your time is appreciated.

Sharon Kizziah-Holmes, thank you for everything. You and Paperback-Press made publishing this trilogy possible. You are a professional in every way.

CHAPTER ONE

Elizabeth said, "Angel, I know she's cute and precious as can be, but we need to be downstairs to meet our ride to the hospital."

I looked at my daughter of eighteen months and then kissed her forehead and gave her over to her nanny. "Take care of Alice and you know how to reach us."

When we reached street level our limo was at the curb waiting for us. Before leaving the building I looked up and down the street for anything suspicious before walking to the car and opening the rear door for my eleven-year-old sister, Elizabeth April Alice Jennifer Barbara Angel Pearson, and then followed her into the car. Her nanny would meet us at Johns Hopkins Hospital later when it was time for Elizabeth to return home. My poor sister had been saddled with the names of all the woman who had anything to do with the establishment of our family line.

Elizabeth was given the gift of healing by touch when she was ten, much like I had when I was five. When I was fifteen I lost that power, but was given other powers instead, including the ability to diagnose illness or injury by touch.

"Angel, how many patients are waiting for me this time?"

"Last night I was told there were six patients. Have you had any recurrence of the pain when you touch a patient to cure them?"

"Look at my hand now. It's completely healed, but I still don't understand why it affected me this way and didn't you when you first started healing people."

I placed my hand over hers and squeezed it slightly. "Elizabeth, I don't understand it either. Just be glad that when I placed my hand over yours when you touched the patient, we both felt a connection and your pain stopped. The only thing I can think of is that I needed to pass the torch on to you. You know we didn't get a book of instructions when we got our powers. We learn as we go."

"Well, I've done at least a dozen since then without pain and best of all, the patients have been healed."

"I talked to Dad yesterday and he informed me my Angel Foundation is now the Elizabeth Foundation. All your income from the hospital goes into the non-profit, tax free foundation. Those patients who can't afford to pay what the hospital charges is taken care of by the foundation."

Rush hour traffic was generally going south, while we were heading north. I had a strange thought. "Elizabeth, I think the birthmarks of a small cross on our backs, which now includes Alice, is God's way of showing our connection to Him."

"You mean in addition to us all looking alike. It's like we are part of a sisterhood serving as His healing hand."

Thirty minutes later our limo pulled into the ER entrance of Johns Hopkins Hospital of Kansas City. Normally I would have checked in at the ER desk, but today Elizabeth and I hung a left and walked down a short hallway to another reception counter whose nurse greeted us.

"Doctor Pearson-Blake, Elizabeth. We have six patients today. Five are adults and one nine year-old boy. Their charts are on the wall outside their rooms beginning at Room 100."

I looked around the reception area checking for security. There were two armed security officers located on either side of the entryway, and three more were inside the ER entryway where we first arrived. Since Elizabeth started healing people and became an item in the news, the crazies had started to gather. For safety's sake we had increased security at the hospital.

Three aides took care of the patients' needs and made them as comfortable as possible while they awaited the arrival of the Healer. The first patient was the child, Russell Lane, who was in the final stage of a rare blood cancer. I knocked and then we entered to find Russell propped up in bed. Previous failed cancer treatments had left him without any hair and his body emaciated to little more than skin over his bones.

Elizabeth immediately went to him and asked, "What's your name?"

He answered in a surprising strong voice, "Russell Lane, but I go by Rusty. Are you the angel that's going to make me well again?"

"We're not angels, but my sister here is named Angel. I'm Elizabeth and I'm here to heal you if God wills it. Are you ready or do you want to say a prayer before I start?"

He held his hand up for a stay as he closed his eyes and prayed. When he finished he opened his eyes. "Good luck for both of us."

Elizabeth stepped to his side and touched his arm. "Heal this boy."

Rusty stiffened as through shocked with an electric current, then he gradually relaxed. He opened his eyes and looked at Elizabeth. "You might not be an angel, but the angel I just saw said I was cured and that you were the reason."

We quickly went through the remaining five patients on whom conventional medicine had failed. After Elizabeth finished healing them, two were immediately released, while the others were admitted as convalescents until their physical condition improved to where they could be released as outpatients.

CHAPTER TWO

I'm still mad at Angel for suggesting that I be named after all the important women in my life, while she named her daughter after only two of them. Alice is the mother of Mom, and April is the mother of Dad, both are my grandmothers. However, I'm really happy they made my first name Elizabeth. She was my favorite great grandmother, not only because we both loved each other, but because she knew all our family's history and freely gave me advice on how to survive.

Early on Grandmother Elizabeth told me that my family was protected from mortal danger by Olivia, a guardian angel. My mother's sister, Barbara, is the other angel that is looking out for us. Barbara died in an car accident shortly after she became engaged to Dad. Her self-portrait is over our mantel and she talks to us sometimes, giving us advice and news of things that will happen in the future. My nanny, Lauren Mays, doesn't know about Barbara yet. Barbara talks to me in my dreams now so we won't frighten Lauren.

Angel's daughter, Alice, is scary powerful and she's only eighteen months old. Yesterday she mentally talked to me. Apparently, I'm the only one she can mentally talk to and her demands are simple so far, just food and changing diapers. When I told Angel what Alice was doing, she asked me to keep her informed.

* * *

I thought to myself, *I'm going to make a notation to have a nervous breakdown this time tomorrow. When Elizabeth told me about Alice mentally talking to her I about lost it. Why me? Is she going to start moving objects with her mind next? I'm going to get with Elizabeth and try to piggyback my thoughts with hers and try to mentally talk with my daughter.*

I gave Elizabeth a package of tampons. "Read the directions and if you don't understand anything let me know, otherwise go into the restroom and use it."

"Well, it looks simple enough. I'll be right back."

Elizabeth had confided on the ride to the hospital that her first period had started this morning. When she returned we went to the ER waiting room where I checked if her ride was waiting on her. Her nanny was waiting for us there and they soon departed for home. It was almost ten a.m. as I made my way to my ER office. I was the department head of Emergency Medicine and Unconventional Medical Treatment. The main hospital's ten floors were divided - the top six floors for conventional patients, then a surgical floor, followed by two floors for unconventional patients. The first floor was ER, reception, and patient rooms for those who have come for healing by Elizabeth. My expertise is for the unconventional medical treatment of patients and the department head of emergency medicine. The new wing of the hospital was for only conventional medical patients.

In addition to the hospital's world class doctors of conventional medicine, they had Elizabeth and my gifts for healing patients. Elizabeth worked on the hopeless cases and I handled those no other surgeon would even attempt. Our conventional cases were performed by world class surgeons, one of which was my husband, Jeff Blake. Johns Hopkins Hospital of Kansas City has earned a well-deserved reputation of the place to send difficult cases.

When I arrived at my office my assistant, Joyce Martin, informed me that Dr. Jacob Holmes, the head of surgery, wished to speak to me. I asked Joyce if I had any fires to put out and at her negative reply I headed towards Dr. Holmes' office after telling her to call ahead that I'm on my way.

His assistant waved me on into his office where I found Jeff talking to Dr. Holmes. Jeff looked up as I entered and quickly gave me a kiss that made my toes curl. "Honey, that one is for not kissing you this morning when I left early. We were just discussing a case that we need your help on. From the confusing symptoms we think our patient has more than one problem. Would you enlighten us?"

I smiled at the two men who looked at me with hopeful expressions. "Sure, I'll make my best effort. Take me to the patient."

The patient was a black woman who was born in west Africa and had been in the United States since she was eight, twelve years ago. She had lived in the Midwest for the last six years and was a computer technician. Her symptoms included a skin rash, high fever, loss of hair, and fingernail discoloration.

I looked at them. "Have you checked for radiation poisoning?"

Dr. Holmes motioned for us to leave the room and follow him to the nurses' station. He asked the head nurse, "Has the blood work arrived yet for patient Umbutu in room 612?"

She handed over the report to Dr. Holmes, whose face quickly turned grim. "Her white cell count is very low. I think you're right Angel, and you didn't even touch her. Nurse, place a radiation quarantine on Room 612, and I need to turn this patient over to another doctor with radiation experience. Surgery was called in when the original diagnose was liver failure, which didn't made sense when we looked at her."

I said, "We all need to take radiation showers and put on new scrubs. Do you know where we have them?"

Jeff said, "I do. But what about the nurses and the others who have been in contact with her?"

Dr. Holmes said, "Nurse Triplett send everyone who had contact with Umbutu to the radiation showers. Someone will be there to make sure a list is maintained. In the meantime no one enters 612 until a new doctor is assigned this case. Call security and have a man placed outside the room to enforce the ban."

When we got to the showers, I modestly let the men go first and would wait my turn. I used my cell to call Dr. Ellsworth, the hospital Administrator, and informed her of our problem. She replied, "I'll notify the proper authorities and have Dr. Kate McQuarry handle the patient. When you get things settled there I want to speak to all three of you in my office."

When Dr. Holmes and Jeff came out of the shower room in new scrubs I told Holmes, "I've already informed Dr. Ellsworth and she wanted to talk to us ASAP. Dr. McQuarry will take over for you on the patient and the authorities will be informed. A nurse should be arriving soon to document who has taken radiation showers."

Four female nurses arrived as I was speaking and when I finished, I motioned for them to follow me into the showers. There were ten shower stalls, so we had plenty of room, but that soon changed as others continued to arrive. When I rejoined my original group we headed towards Dr. Ellsworth office. I counted her as a good friend and we've shared lots of history. While at the Johns Hopkins University she was my faculty advisor and then during my residency at the hospital she passed messages to me from the President of the Johns Hopkins organization. She was now the Hospital Administrator and my supervisor.

We were immediately shown into her office by her secretary. Dr. Ellsworth pointed at the seating area. "Sit and tell me how this happened."

She looked at us. "Well? Somebody start talking. Angel, you called me so give me the story from your prospective."

I gave her the story from start to finish and then shut my mouth. Dr. Ellsworth looked at Dr. Holmes and crooked her eyebrow. "Well, it's your turn now."

"Janice, I've been away from general medicine too long. Angel didn't even touch the patient before asking if I'd checked for radiation poisoning. The patient was sent to me as a possible liver failure, but Jeff said it didn't look right so I sent for Angel."

"Who referred the patient to you?"

"Dr. Jason Witherspoon. He's a recent hire."

"Okay, first thing that shouldn't have happened. There should have been two doctors who agreed on the diagnose before she was transferred to you, or Jeff in this case. He realized something was amiss and sent for Angel, who immediately recognized the symptoms. Her eidetic memory no doubt helped her in that regard. Angel, you may return to your duties, while the boy's and I try to get to the bottom of this fiasco."

I patted Jeff's shoulder as I left the room. I was glad Dr. Witherspoon was not one of my ER doctors, but I still could use him as an example of what not to do at my next meeting. I returned to my office for a short catch-up on paperwork time, then checked on my new residents in the ER.

They had been on the job for only two days and I wanted to be sure of their abilities before I gave them any responsibilities. Taylor Upton and Hanna Wilson had high marks in medical school, but they needed to prove themselves to me. Taylor was twenty-seven, tall for a woman at six feet, had a killer body with brunette hair, and was a product of Dallas, Texas. Hanna was the same age, but was six inches shorter with blond hair and a slim athletic body to match, from Springfield, Missouri.

Dr. Ellsworth had warned me earlier that I was getting a lot of interest from interns based upon the rumors they had heard about my history while attending medical school and residency at Johns Hopkins. However, these two appeared to have selected this location because it was close to their homes.

Their supervisor, Dr. Joe Grimes, was putting them through my training program where I got to observe them in action as a patient was wheeled into the ER. The young male patient was in a neck brace and had inflatable casts on his left arm and right leg. He appeared to be about twelve years old and had cuts on his face and body evidenced by his bloody clothing. He was not completely awake and was moaning in pain. Dr. Grimes took what history was available from the EMT's, who then left. Grimes had Taylor cut the clothes off the boy, while Hanna tended to the bleeding cuts as Grimes checked for other injuries.

Dr. Grimes said, "He appears to have rib damage in addition to the broken arm and leg. Hanna, you and Taylor take him to radiology and let's determine how bad the breaks are. Hanna, stay with him until that's done and then bring him back here with the results. Taylor, hot foot it back here in case I need you while she's gone."+

* * *

Taylor had just returned to the ER when the patient opened his eyes. "Oh crap that hurts! Where am I?"

I said, "You're at Johns Hopkins Hospital and I'm your resident doctor. You're about to get x-rays to check on your broken bones. What's your name?"

"Peter Grayson. Oh my that really smarts. Can you give me something for the pain?"

"No yet. Where does it hurt?"

"My left arm and right leg and it hurts to breathe too."

"Hang on and grit your teeth. Don't move now, I have to leave while they take pictures."

After the x-rays were completed I returned to his side. "Peter, who are your parents and their phone number?"

Peter looked at me in confusion at first, then his eyes started tearing up as he cried, "They were with me in the car!"

"Tell me their names and I'll check to see if they were taken somewhere else."

"Peter and Sally Grayson. I have a older sister, Pamela Hicks, who lives in St. Louis. I don't know her number."

"Take it easy. I'm getting your x-rays and we're going back to the ER."

* * *

I followed Hanna and her patient back to the ER and watched while she gave her report to Dr. Grimes, then all three doctors reviewed the x-rays. Finding no other problems other than the broken bones of his arm, leg, and cracked ribs. They removed the temporary casts and checked for any problems before washing the skin over the breaks and replacing the casts. The ER aides washed him carefully and placed him in a rib support wrap before admitting him into the hospital.

Dr. Grimes gave me the names of the patient's parents and an older sister. I told him Hanna performed great, now it was Taylor's turn. I then returned to my office to determine his parents fate before contacting the boy's sister.

Later that day I visited Peter in his room and introduced myself. "Peter, I have some bad news for you. You were the only survivor of your car crash. I've contacted your sister, Pamela, and she will be here tomorrow to see you. Is there anything I can do for you in the meantime?"

Peter's eyes were full of tears. "I've seen you on TV and you seem to speak to angels. Please put in a good word for my parents and I'll pray too."

I squeezed his shoulder and kissed his forehead before saying, "I'll talk to my aunt tonight. She seems to have the ear of God. Anything else?"

"That resident doctor sure was nice. Could she stop by and see me when she has the time?"

"I believe you are thinking of Hanna Wilson. A resident doesn't have much free time to socialize, but I'll let her know you asked about her."

CHAPTER THREE

That evening when Jeff and I returned to our penthouse apartment and checked in at the security desk at our floor, I was thankful that my parents had given us this apartment which had previously been used to mail out the healing pictures of me to the world. My parents owned the other penthouse apartment on this floor, but theirs had a view of the Plaza. The security in place was originally for me, but now it covered everyone who lived in the two apartments.

We entered our apartment and checked with Grace about Alice before our nanny departed. I picked up my daughter and sat with her in the living room while Jeff prepared supper for us. Alice smiled at me as I played with her, but she seemed a little distracted by something. After dinner it was Jeff's turn to play with our daughter while I cleaned up the dinner mess.

The next day when I arrived at the hospital there was a message waiting on me to see Dr. Ellsworth ASAP. I checked my calendar for other commitments before leaving my office. Dr. Ellsworth's secretary showed me into her office where I took a seat.

Dr. Ellsworth looked at me considering for a moment. "That patient with radioactive poisoning is in a comma, which makes it very difficult to determine where she came into contact with it. A team from the Atomic Energy Agency will be here later this morning, but without the victim alive and talking, about all they can determine is the dose she received."

"You want me or Elizabeth to intervene?"

"I was thinking of Elizabeth. Can you do anything to cure her?"

"If either of us cures her, you will lose your forensic evidence unless you take photographs of the patient's body and retain all your lab results. I think that if I give her one cc of my blood, she will be cured. If not, I'll bring Elizabeth in to do the job."

"If I remember correctly the last time you did this you used a pint of your blood."

"Remember, I got my hand slapped for doing that. I believe one cc of my blood won't get me a scolding from God as long as it's for a good cause."

"Let's talk to Dr. McQuarry and get this done before the patient dies."

We found Dr. McQuarry in her office and after hearing what we were going to do, she led us to the lab where she drew my blood and gave it to the patient. When she rejoined us I asked about the retention of forensic evidence for the investigators from the Atomic Energy Agency.

"I already got all that yesterday. I'm curious on how well this treatment works. Her exposure was enough to kill her, and I hope it works because I don't think we have enough time to call in Elizabeth if it doesn't."

Less than an hour later the investigators arrived and wanted to see the patient. Dr. Ellsworth told them, "Patient Umbutu had been in a comma and close to death when Dr. Angel Pearson-Blake gave her one cc of her blood as a treatment. We may not have had time for any positive results, but let's check."

Everyone suited up, except me, and entered Umbutu's room. I waited outside for about thirty minutes until they all returned and removed their protective suits. Dr. McQuarry said, "It's amazing! She was awake and her vitals were all improved from what they were before the treatment. Angel, these are Agents Mike Lutz and Holly Fursa and they want to ask you about your treatment."

"Since she was awake, did you learn anything about how she was exposed?"

"She didn't know, but we got a list of the places she visited during the three days before she was admitted," said Agent Fursa.

Agent Lutz said, "Dr. Ellsworth told us that when you were a young girl you had the ability to heal by touch, but had since lost that ability and acquired other powers. Your blood appears to have the power to cure at least some illnesses, but God has instructed you to use this gift sparingly. Is this true?"

"Yes. The properties in my blood were meant to protect me from illness."

Agent Fursa said, "Your younger sister Elizabeth now has this ability to heal by touch. Why not use her?"

"She's only eleven and I try not to bring her here for healing sessions unless there are at least six patients needing treatment. In any case, we didn't have time to bring her here this morning."

Agent Lutz asked Dr. Ellsworth, "Is there an office we can use while we are in Kansas City?"

"Yes, I can convert a patient room here on the first floor or place you near Dr. McQuarry on the sixth floor."

"Dr. Pearson-Blake, where is your office located?"

"On the first floor near the ER."

The agents looked at each other and Agent Fursa held up one finger. Agent Lutz said, "We'll take an office on the first floor."

That night as Jeff and I were preparing for bed I told him of the experiences I had with the radiation sickness patient and the two Atomic Energy Agency agents.

"Sounds to me like they want to keep a close watch on what you do. Maybe they're just fascinated with you, I know I am."

I gave him a long passionate kiss as a reward for his comment, then said, "I better check on Alice and make sure the monitor is turned on."

Alice had long since outgrown her crib and was now sleeping in a bed with railings. I wasn't sure how much longer it would be before she would be climbing out of this bed. She appeared to be asleep, but as I was leaving her room I mentally heard her say, *"Bye mommy."*

I did a double-take as I looked back at Alice, then tried to mentally talk to her. *"Alice, was that you talking to me?"*

"Yes. Why didn't you answer me before?"

"I'm sorry honey, but my gifts aren't as strong as what you and Elizabeth have. Can I get you anything before we go to

sleep?"

"No. Bye."

I leaned over and kissed her forehead before leaving the room. Once in my bedroom I crawled over the bed until I was lying on top of Jeff and whispered, "Alice is mentally talking to Elizabeth and me. What do you think of that?"

Jeff's eye's got big. "You're not shitting me are you?"

I kissed his nose. "Nope. Her mental word choices appear far advanced, like something a six year old would say."

"Maybe are minds are translating what she says into something we can understand. This is unusual for an eighteen month-old, even for your family."

"I hope you said that as a compliment."

"Yes dear. You know we need to consult with Barbara on this, and the sooner the better. Let's take some personal time tomorrow morning and see what we can find out."

Alice was now sleeping until seven a.m., which was their wakeup call the next morning. I took care of Alice and gave her the usual bottle of formula. As she was working on that I mentally asked her, *"Do you want fruit or oatmeal next?"*

"Fruit tastes better."

"Okay, but your body needs oatmeal too. I'll make sure Grace gives you that later today."

"Jeff, would you call Grace Simpson and tell her to come in two hours later than usual?"

"Already did that. Pancakes are about ready, how about you?"

"Mommy can I have pancakes too?"

"I'll let you have some of mine. Now be still while I dress."

After we finished breakfast and did the cleanup, we all sat before the photograph of Barbara's self-portrait. The original was still in my parents' apartment. I said, "Barbara, we need a little guidance here. Alice is now mentally taking to Elizabeth and me, but not Jeff yet. Is there anything we should be aware of that we need to be doing?"

Barbara seemed to step out of her picture and stood before us. "My, Alice is powerful for her age. She's going to develop other powers as she gets older. You can't hide what she is from her nanny any longer. If she can't handle it, you need to get someone who can. You need to give Alice guidelines on what is acceptable behavior because she eventually will start to move things with her mind. Show her how to use a computer and let her learn about the world around her, much like you and Elizabeth did. Any questions?"

Both Jeff and I sat with our mouths open in panic, then I stood with Alice in my arms and gave my aunt a level look. "Barbara, is this something we can handle without going bonkers?"

"Angel, you are the glue that is going to tie you three together for what is to come. Suck it up. I think you're going to like what's coming."

Barbara picked Alice up out of my arms and kissed her forehead, then looked intently into Alice's eyes for a few minutes before handing her back to me. She then disappeared back into the photograph.

I asked Alice, *"What did Aunt Barbara say to you?"*

"She told me to follow your instructions because my new powers may harm others if they are not properly controlled."

"Alice, you know your father and I love you very much and we would not knowingly harm you in any way. If you discover a new power, like being able to move objects with your mind, let us know so that we can work with you in its proper use."

"Why does daddy not hear my mental voice like you do?"

"He doesn't have powers like you, Elizabeth, and I do. Maybe we can think of something that will let him hear your mental voice."

"I will think on it, but will talk with you before doing anything."

"Pay attention to what your nanny says when we inform her that you are special. If she leaves we will have to find another nanny."

It wasn't long before Grace Simpson arrived and took a seat at our request. I said, "Grace, we've been very happy with your care of Alice, but it's time we tell you a secret about her. You've told us about how advanced she is compared to others of her age you cared for. Well, she is now mentally talking to me and Elizabeth and we've been told that she will soon come into other powers, such as mentally moving objects. Do you still want to care for Alice now that you know what is coming?"

Grace came over and picked up Alice. "Angel, I knew when I

took this job it wasn't going to be like any I've had before. Alice has been a wonder to care for and now you tell me it's really going to get interesting. She and I have already worked out a code when she wants me to do something for her and she doesn't give me a bit of grief. Alice and I have bonded, so you will have to fire me to get rid of me."

Jeff spoke. "Grace, your salary is now doubled because you are now at risk from outside forces as soon as they become aware of Alice's abilities. Be sure to abide by the security procedures entering and leaving the apartment building and be aware of your surroundings."

Later, I checked on the condition of Umbutu as soon as I arrived at the hospital. Dr. McQuarry beamed at me. "I just checked on her blood work and her white cell count is almost normal again. Her skin rash has cleared up and I've released her from quarantine. Do you want to see her?"

When we walked into Umbutu's room I was struck by her improved appearance. Dr. McQuarry introduced me and Umbutu's eyes widened in surprise and delight. "You saved my life! I guess I'm only another person you've saved, but I'll remember you for the rest of my life."

I smiled at her and placed my hand out for her to shake. Instead of immediately releasing her hand I held it tightly for about a minute. After I released her hand I said, "Sorry about that, but I wanted to scan your body to see how your body was healing itself. I do remember everyone I take a personal interest in, and my treatment will have a lasting effect upon your body. Barring an accident, you will have a long life without illness. I hope you use this long life to better yourself and those around you."

Umbutu looked at me with unshed tears in her eyes. "I pledge to you that I will work to earn this gift you have given me. If you need me for anything, don't hesitate to ask."

I smiled at her and kissed her cheek, then gave her my card. "Call me if you need my help."

After we left her room and walking down the hallway, I said, "At this rate of recovery I expect her to be ready for release within a week. Try to keep her on an annual checkup so that we can monitor her health as long as possible. Tell her it's at my request and she may continue with it even if she moves out of the area."

"How many have you done like this?"

"This is the second one and they were both females. Check with Dr. Ellsworth and get the information on the other patient. I think we should handle these and any others from here. Please ask Dr. Ellsworth to get someone permanently assigned this task."

A loud yell brought my attention to three men struggling with the two security officers at the elevators. "Quick! Call for more security and then get out of sight," I said as I moved to meet the threat.

The three attackers left the security officers bleeding on the floor and turned my way, but hesitated as they saw me approaching them. Apparently, the attackers didn't see me as a threat to them as they continued toward me with deadly intent. A blinding flash of light appeared between me and the attackers. Olivia extended her wings and her sword flashed lightning, engulfing them in flame until they were only three body husks on the floor. She turned to me and I saluted her, then she disappeared in another flash of light.

I hurried to the two security officers lying on the floor to check their condition and give aid if needed. The male officer was dead; however, the female officer was alive, but unconscious. The elevator door opened and six more security officers burst into the hallway and took in their surroundings.

I informed them of my identity and that the threat was over. I pointed at the body husks down the hallway. "Those were the attackers that my guardian angel took care of. I think their target was Ms. Umbutu in room 625. She needs two officers outside her room and three more at the elevators. The agents from the Atomic Energy Agency may want to take additional measures later."

Dr. McQuarry arrived with two nurses and they quickly loaded the unconscious officer onto a gurney and took her to the ER.

I asked the security officers, "Who's senior?"

A older man stepped forward. "That's me doctor. My name is Sgt. Peterson."

"Well Sergeant as you well know this is now a crime scene. Put cones around those three bodies and a sheet over the downed officer. Keep all your officers here until released by the police when they get here. Has anyone called 911?"

"No one from my group."

"Okay, I'll let the hospital administrator do the honors."

I pulled out my cell and called Dr. Ellsworth telling her what had just happened and as far as we knew no one had called 911 yet. I then said, "The Atomic Energy agents should be notified as their patient appeared to be the target."

"Crap! Okay, you did good. I'll take care of the rest."

I looked at Sgt. Peterson. "Why don't you send some of your people to the break room and bring back coffee for everyone. I prefer milk with mine."

CHAPTER FOUR

Fifteen minutes later the first police officers arrived and consulted with Sgt. Peterson. The police Sergeant raised his eyebrows, then looked at the three dead bodies and then at me. Ten minutes later two detectives arrived and talked to the Sergeant's before heading my way. Both detectives were women and introduced themselves as Detectives May North and Jane Kirkpatrick.

Det. North asked, "You burn those guys?"

I gave her a small smile. "That's not one of my powers. My guardian angel did that. I can probably save you some time. Contact Det. Ed Patterson and Det. Florence Snyder of the Baltimore PD. They have experience with my angels. My mother and father also have had similar incidents that the Kansas City PD investigated."

Det. Kirkpatrick asked, "Your maiden name is Pearson, Angel Pearson? May, she's the one that's been on the news. She used to be a healer and now has other powers. Let's take everyone's statements and let the front office handle this."

Two hours later I was sitting in Dr. Ellsworth's office waiting for her to finish talking with President Smithson, who was head of the Johns Hopkins organization. I was zoning out waiting my turn with Dr. Ellsworth, when the words, "Yes, she's here with me," brought me alert.

Dr. Ellsworth put it on speaker mode before handing the cell phone to me with an expressionless face. "This is Angel, what can I do for you President Smithson."

"Have you ruled out that those men were not after you?"

"Not 100%, but logic would indicate it was a patient they were after. If I was the target I think they would have picked a better place to attack me."

"That's our thought as well. Apparently your guardian angel is still on the job. From my report you didn't hesitate to confront those men. You that confident in your defensive powers?"

"Sir, I haven't told you of all my powers that I've learned to use. If Olivia hadn't shown up, maybe we would have had someone to interrogate."

"That's good to know. How is Elizabeth holding up? Any problems there?"

"So far she's doing great. My problem is with my daughter. At eighteen months she's starting to talk to me mentally. She's a very strong individual and Aunt Barbara tells me she will soon start mentally moving objects."

Dr. Ellsworth audibly inhaled, while there was shocked silence from Smithson's end for a few moments. "Do you think she will follow your instructions?"

"Yes, Aunt Barbara is involved and Alice loves us. It's just a little stressful for Jeff and me right now."

"I don't know what we can do to help, but if you think of anything let us know."

Dr. Ellsworth concluded the call and disconnected before turning to me. "Angel, you certainly led an interesting life."

"Unfortunately not just me, but everyone associated with me. I guess I was never meant to have a boring life. Have you heard what the AEA agents plan on doing now that their witness has been threatened?"

Dr. Ellsworth gave me a quirky smile before saying, "I think they are more interested in you than her, but they have sent for U.S. Marshalls to take over her protection. They should be arriving later today."

"I guess I had better get back to work if you don't have anything else."

"No, just stay safe."

When I got back to the ER the first person I checked in with was Head Nurse Lilly Cox, my black roommate during our undergraduate years at MU of Columbia, Missouri. She was my first and best friend after I left home for school and we conspired together so that we could work together again after she completed nursing school. Lilly met and later married Robert Cox, who is also a nurse. I encouraged them to train as ER nurses and settle near Kansas City, as those were the cryptic clues my Aunt Barbara had given me.

Lilly saw me heading her way and rushed to meet me. "I've been worried about you since they brought that security officer to us. So, Olivia saved your butt again. What did the police think about your explanation of a guardian angel taking the bad guys out?"

"Oh, they bumped that problem upstairs. They just took my statement and let me go, at least for now. What's the condition of the security officer?"

"She took a hit to her head and has a slight concussion. They sent her home and told her to take it easy for three days and then report back here for a checkup before returning to work. Let me look at you, how are you coping?"

I smiled at her. "I see you're in your mother hen mode. I'm fine, I think I could have taken those guy's if Olivia hadn't shown up, but her help was appreciated."

"Yeah, you need a guardian angel the risks you take. Oh, oh, here comes Bob. You want me to handle him?"

I stepped behind Lilly and said, "She made me do it!"

Bob Cox's frown turned to an flustered expression. "Dang it Angel. Must you put yourself at risk like that? It's a wonder they don't assign two guardian angels to protect you. Lilly was about to have kittens when we heard what happened. You know we love you, so don't make us worry about you so much."

"Okay, I'll try. You know I'm playing this by ear and I'm mostly reacting to what's happening around me. It's nice to have close friends who really care about me. Is everything going smooth in the ER?"

Lilly snickered. "Like a fine watch. Even the new residents have found their groove."

"Do either one of them show any bias toward you two?"

"No, they are professional. I don't think they would invite us to dinner though."

"Have you made any close friends here in the hospital besides me?"

Lilly said, "A few of both sexes in the nursing staff. Angel, there's some of the doctors and nurses who are scared of you because of the rumors and what they have observed. However, if you were to ask them to jump, most of the staff would say how high."

"Because they were scared of me?"

"No, most like you. You have a leadership quality that draws other people to you. I saw it when we were together in school and you were only a snot-nosed fifteen year old. I've heard stories about you while you were in Johns Hopkins University and later as a resident in the hospital. You bloomed there and were like a bright light attracting others to you."

"Maybe, but I had my conflicts there too."

"Those conflicts are what fueled your mystique. There are no staff members that doesn't know about your self-defense Judo class beating a bunch of men attacking them with no harm to class members. I know of ten staff members who are now taking Judo."

I said, "Wow, maybe we can have classes here paid by the hospital."

I pulled my cell and called Dr. Ellsworth. Fifteen minutes later I found Lilly and Bob. "Pass the word that next month free self-defense Judo classes are going to start at the hospital. Everyone who's interested should sign up at human resources."

That evening on the drive home Jeff quizzed me on my eventful day. After I finished, he smiled. "My, another day in the life of Angel Pearson-Blake. By the way I heard about your free Judo classes starting next month."

"What! I'm not teaching them. Dr. Ellsworth said she'd bring in instructors as needed."

"Maybe so, but the staff wants you there to start it off and give your seal of approval."

"Well, that's all right then. I haven't got time to teach even one class, but I would like to train for a higher level black belt. How about you. I saw a little hint of flab this morning in the shower."

"Where?"

"Right here." I jabbed him in the ribs.

"Okay, we'll have a contest on who improves the most in a month's time, judged by our instructor. The winner gets a back rub every night for a week."

"No fair. You have more muscle to rub. If I win I get two weeks."

When we got home, Grace reported nothing unusual with her charge. I picked Alice up and kissed her on the cheek, while Jeff locked up after Grace left. I mentally asked Alice, *"Anything new to report?"*

"No disturbance in the force detected."

"Dang it. Has Grace been watching Star Wars?"

"She thought I would enjoy it. I have an idea on how to bring daddy into our mental conversations. Have him touch me or you while we are talking."

"Okay, but that sounds too simple."

"Jeff, Alice tells me that if you touch either her or me while we mentally talk you may be able to join in."

Jeff came over to where we were standing and touched my arm. *"Daddy, can you hear me?"*

"Yes honey. How about you, can you hear me?"

"Good! Now we all can talk to each other through this arrangement. Mommy, I can feel my brain expand each time I use it like this. Is my head getting bigger?"

"No dear. Your awareness is expanding, not your actual brain. Can you tell what I'm thinking when I'm not talking to you?"

"I can't tell the difference. Try to block your thoughts. Yes, that did it. Apparently, we can do that."

"Your mind was always blank to us until you started talking to us, so you must have a natural block in place."

"Wow, I think you're right. Mommy, I'm hungry and I need a change. This is nasty. How much longer do I have to put up with this?"

"Not as long as I had to since you're already walking, maybe another three months if you concentrate real hard."

"Put the potty where I can get to it. I'm going to try reaching it before I go."

"Have you been able to do that before?"

"No."

"Well, keep trying and eventually you'll make it."

"Yes mommy."

"Okay, formula then fruit cup?"

"Yes. How soon can I stop that oatmeal, that's yucky."

"I'll check on that for you and get back to you. Maybe you can eat adult oatmeal with sugar and toast?"

"Angel, I think that's too soon for her digestive tract, but let's check what we can change."

"Hear that, daddy's on it too."

That night as we lay together in each other's arms, I thought, *"Oh this is nice lying together like this and smelling my man's natural musk."*

"Careful what you think because I'm connected to you now when we are touching."

"So April doesn't have to be touching us for this work. Mmm, I think I like this. However, right now all I want is a good night's sleep."

The next morning I was in my office less than thirty minutes when the two AEA agents visited me. Agent Lutz took the lead with his question. "Dr. Pearson-Blake, why is it that whenever something happens here you are always at its center?"

"Is there a question somewhere in that statement?"

"Yes. What were you doing in our patient's room?"

"I assume you are talking about Mary Umbutu. If so Dr. McQuarry and I were checking her vitals since the treatment I gave her, and I was making arrangements to follow her progress after she leaves the hospital."

"What's this baloney about your guardian angel killing those men?"

"Well, I didn't do it and there were witnesses, besides I don't own a ray gun."

I turned to Agent Fursa. "You better contact your office because I think your partner is delusional."

I thought Agent Lutz was going to stroke out as his face turned an interesting shade of purple, and he took a step towards me sputtering words without any meaning to me until Agent Fursa stood in front him and slapped his face. The slap did its job and he seemed to come to his senses, whereupon Agent Fursa led him away.

Julie, my office assistant, giggled when they were far enough away so that they couldn't hear her. I couldn't help but give a little smile myself. "Now what was I doing before that interruption?"

"You have a meeting with your ER doctors in ten minutes."

After my weekly meeting with my staff doctors I did a walk through the ER to get a feel of how things were working. I stopped and talked to Lilly about how the two residents were doing from a nurse's prospective and got positive reviews for both of them. I noticed that they both were following me with their eyes as I moved around the room and I suspected they knew of my friendship with Lilly and her husband. If they were smart they would have cultivated a friendship with both of them.

CHAPTER FIVE

I stopped and started walking toward them. "Doctors. I have a question for each of you. The one who gives me the correct answer before the other gets a reward. Are you ready?"

At their uncertain nods I said, "You are the doctor in charge of the ER and all other teams are busy with patients. What would you do if two new patients arrive, one who is in apparent cardiac arrest and the other with severe trauma but currently stable."

Dr. Wilson said, "I would initially try to get the cardiac arrest patient stable since the other is stable."

Dr. Upton said, "I agree."

"You both are correct, but Dr. Wilson was the first. Now for your reward. I think I'll give you a choice. Door number one is three extra hours off and door number two is you may follow me around the hospital tomorrow watching me work."

"I'll take door number two. Where and what time do I meet you?"

"Are you sure you want to do this? It might not be as exciting as yesterday."

"Are you kidding me? You seem to draw excitement to you."

"Okay, meet me in my office in the morning at eight. Oh, oh here comes in some more work for you. Better get cracking or Dr. Dias will be on your case."

They hurried to the gurney the EMT's were rolling into the

ER, with Taylor Upton saying, "I'll give you my next break time if I can take your place tomorrow."

"No thanks, but I'll give you a first-hand report on what happens."

"They must be getting bored to want to tag along with me."

I checked in with Dr. Ellsworth and reported what had happened between me and the AEA agents and asked if there had been any blow back yet.

"No. But I wanted to ask you for recommendations for Judo instructors. It may be difficult to get them to come to the hospital."

"I'll check with my parents and see what they know. It's been almost twelve years since I've had any formal instruction, so my contacts are outdated. Has anyone shown any interest in taking the class yet?"

"It's only been one day and thirty-one have already signed up. I bet we get twenty percent of the staff at this rate."

"That's encouraging. If we have enough students to have daily classes, we can dedicate a room for that purpose and leave the mats on the floor. Before I try to contact anyone to act as our instructor, let's see how many sign up this week so that I can better judge what our needs will be."

After I returned to my office I called Dad. "Dad, the hospital is going to start free Judo classes next month and I was hoping you know someone I can contact for instructors."

"Wait a sec while I check if I have his number. Here it is - Master Yow at the Greater Kansas City Martial Arts Center. You better make an appointment and speak to him in person as he doesn't do well with telephone conversations."

"Okay, let me have the number and I'll do that."

The earliest appointment available was next Monday afternoon at three. The address was in Liberty, north of the Missouri River, not that far from the hospital if I use the interstate. I informed Dr. Ellsworth of the appointment. "May we use the conference room in the new wing. I think we need it if we have over ten students at each session. If we need the room for a conference it can be converted back to its original purpose with little effort."

"That sounds like a good plan, but let's not do anything else until we know we're going to have instructors."

I called the nurse station covering Mary Umbutu and asked if the Marshalls were still outside her door. Getting a yes answer, I was satisfied that she was protected and continued my normal day.

When I arrived at my office the following day, Dr. Hanna Wilson was waiting. "Take a chair while I see what's on my schedule today."

Fifteen minutes later I started my rounds in the ER talking to each of the doctors, solving their problems and making notes to myself. Before I left the ER I asked Dr. Wilson, "What would you change in the ER?"

Hanna looked at me in surprise. "Why do we make sure all unconscious patients are restrained before they enter the ER?"

"In Baltimore we used to get druggies coming in that way and sometimes they would wake up and attack the staff. I haven't had that problem here since we use restraints."

"Oh, that makes sense. I can't think of anything else."

I led the way to the nurse's desk for Elizabeth's patients. I asked for a list of waiting patients and as she handed it to me said, "We have seven patients, one juvenile and six adults. We expect three more this afternoon by one o'clock."

"Okay, I'll arrange for Elizabeth to be here at three to take care of whoever is here then. Make arrangements to place the newest arrivals last on her schedule."

I gave her back the list and Hanna followed me to the surgical floor to Dr. Holmes' office. He looked up as we entered. "Whose your shadow?"

"Resident Doctor Wilson, this fascinating man is Chief of Surgery Dr. Jacob Holmes. Dr. Wilson is following me around today as a reward for answering a question correctly. Jacob, do you have any residents?"

"Not yet. I hear you have two. How come you are so blessed?"

"I got the pick of the litter. Ten asked for service with me, but only gave me two. Talk to Janice, I mean Dr. Ellsworth, if you want some. I'll bet she can arrange it. Your message said that you had need of my services?"

"Yes, one of your ER young female patients with compound fractures will have severe scarring. Do you want to do your magic?"

"Do you mind if Dr. Wilson observes?"

"Not at all. I'll have my nurse take you to her room."

Nurse Jill Black gave us background information on the patient as we walked. "Marilyn Wasson is twenty-two, single, and attending KU. Both of her legs had compound fractures."

When we entered her room and I introduced myself, Marilyn's face seemed to brighten. "You're the angel doctor who performs miracles'."

I looked at Hanna and shook my head. "Sorry, my name is Angel and I'm not an angel. Let me look at your wounds and I'll see what I can do for you."

After uncovering the legs I placed my hand on each leg, fusing the bones together at the breaks and repaired severed blood vessels and muscle tissue. I then brought the skin tissue together and fused it until only a thin red line was visible. I turned to the nurse, whose mouth was still open in awe, and said, "Her legs are no longer broken and starting tomorrow she needs to start walking again, slow at first, but as her muscles heal she should walk longer. I'll be back tomorrow to check on her."

Marilyn said, "Doctor please come here so that I can talk to you in private."

Marilyn's face was streaked with tears as I bent close to her head. "You may not be an angel, but you do miracles that only someone touched by God can do. Thank you for giving me back my life that I thought was lost to me. I was a great tennis player, now at least I can play again."

"Remember what I gave you and try to make someone else's life better when the opportunity arises."

Marilyn squeezed my hand and I left the room with my shadow who said, "Doctor, I've heard of your doing something similar to what you did in there, but I guess I thought they were overstating what happened. That's a gift and not something you can teach me is it?"

"No, I can't teach you how to do that. My gift of healing by touch has not entirely left me as I first thought. Elizabeth touches a person and whatever is wrong is healed. I touch a person and I can feel what is wrong within their body and usually I can make changes by using my mind to correct the problem."

"Wow, that's an awesome ability. Forgive me Doctor, but you don't appear to be an elitist, one who thinks they are better than others around you. In fact, you go out of your way to help others succeed. Maybe that's why we are drawn to you, like moths to a flame."

"Dr. Wilson, what do you see when you look at me."

"A beautiful woman whose white hair seems to give you an exotic look. But what I didn't see when I first met you, but is now apparent to me, is a faint purple glow around you that I think is your aura. When you were attending to Marilyn Wasson, your aura became darker and faded when you finished."

"I haven't heard anyone else mention seeing my aura, but several did say I seemed to glow. Oh well, I better arrange for Elizabeth to be here this afternoon."

After making the necessary calls I led us back to the ER break room. By chance Dr. Taylor Upton was just sitting down when we arrived and after getting our drink of choice we joined her at her table. Dr. Wilson asked, "May I tell Taylor about what you did for Ms. Wasson?"

At my nod, she started telling her what she observed. Dr. Upton glanced my way several times as if to gauge whether this story was valid, but at its end her mouth was open in awe.

Dr. Upton said, "Dr. Pearson-Blake please let me tag along when you do another of those procedures. It will give me bragging rights the next time I'm with other doctors. They may not believe me, but I'll know it happened."

I smiled at her. "We'll see. It will depend on the workload."

I fell into a relaxed state and only heard my residents' voices as noise without comprehending what was being said. Several minutes passed before Dr. Wilson touched my arm and repeated calling my name, bringing me back to the present.

"Yes, what did you say?"

"Dr. Ellsworth wants you in her office ASAP."

My shadow and I hurried to the Administrator's office where Dr. Wilson was told to wait outside while I entered to find Dr. Ellsworth was not alone. I smiled at the two Secret Service agents. "Agent's Jackson Bourne and Beverly Graham. What brings you back to Kansas City?"

Bourne handed Graham a twenty dollar bill, which she snapped between her hands and winked at me. "I'll give you your half later. I told him about your eidetic memory, but he said after so much time there was no way you could remember our names."

Bourne cleared his throat, bringing us back to the point of the meeting. "The First Lady will be giving a talk next month in the Kansas City area and we wanted to be brought up to date on the status of your ER and surgery department."

"Would you like the Chief of Surgery present for this review?"

"Yes, both the hospital's ER and Surgery departments have gained many accolades since our last review. Why not give us a walking tour of the ER on our way to Dr. Holmes' office. I'm sure Dr. Ellsworth will let him know we are on our way to see him."

I introduced Dr. Wilson as one of our two ER residents who was shadowing me today and asked if she could join us. Agent Bourne smiled at her. "It's perfect. We can ask her questions from her perspective."

Hanna and I exchanged worried looks as we walked towards the ER. Agent Graham asked, "Dr. Wilson how long have you been a resident here?"

"Three months ma'am."

"Where do you call home?"

"Springfield, Missouri. That's about four hours by car."

"So you wanted to do your residency here because it's close to your home?"

"No ma'am. That's a benefit, but the reason is that I wanted to work with Dr. Pearson-Blake. She's a legend back in Baltimore."

"So you went to medical school at Johns Hopkins as well? By legend, what do you mean?"

"Her records of accomplishments while she attended medical school and residency are outstanding. Everything she attempted she was the top performer. She started a self-defense class in Judo, which was later attacked by a bunch of men who were subdued by her and three brown belts. There were no injuries suffered by the students, but all but one of the attackers had broken arms."

"Dr. Pearson-Blake, I wasn't aware that you knew Judo. When did you receive your training?"

"I received my black belt when I was fifteen."

"That's about the time you started undergraduate work at MU in Columbia, Missouri. Three years later you started medical school at Johns Hopkins. That's quite an accomplishment."

"An eidetic memory and a genus IQ helps quite a lot, but I had a goal given to me by God that I was working toward."

We reached the ER and I started explaining how patients were treated from the moment they came through the doors until they were given treatment and released or admitted to the hospital. We currently only have one patient being treated, but can work on eight at one time by calling in doctors from the hospitals staff. Normally we have two ER doctors for each shift which can handle the work load ninety percent of the time. Also, I pitch in and help as needed."

The agents didn't have any questions, so I led the group toward the elevators. Dr. Holmes met us on his floor when the doors opened. I reintroduced the agents to him and he began a tour of the surgery suites. We were soon joined by Jeff who was introduced as my husband and the lead surgeon.

Agent Graham said, "The last time we were here you were the resident surgeon that showed great promise. You seem to have fulfilled that promise. How many surgeons are on staff?"

"Eighteen, but that doesn't include our greatest surgeon. Angel worked on a patient earlier today that had both legs with compound fractures. She had asked us to let her know if any patients had injuries that would leave excessive scarring. She not only repaired the broken bones, torn blood vessels, and muscle tissue, but her legs only show a faint red line where the injuries occurred."

Agent Bourne said, "May we see the patient?"

When we got to Marilyn Wasson's room I stopped everyone. "I want to get Marilyn's permission for this show and tell, otherwise the hospital might get sued."

I entered her room. "Marilyn, two Secret Service agents are here to review the hospital's ability to care for members of the first family and they want to talk to you and view your wounds. Would you give your permission?"

Marilyn smiled. "Of course. Send them in."

After everyone had entered the room I asked, "Are you in any pain?"

"No, only a twinge when I move my legs."

I removed the covers over her legs. "Please wiggle your toes for me."

After several more tasks were completed I asked her to swing her legs off the bed and slowly stand on her legs. Without hesitation she sat on the edge of the bed and I offered her my arm for support as she stood.

"Any pain now?"

"No pain, but my feet tingle a little."

"Take three steps toward Dr. Holmes and I'll help you if you need it."

Marilyn took her first step, then a second, and with a big smile took her third, turned and walked back to the bad. "Wow, I'm walking. I heard you tell the nurse to start me walking tomorrow, but this is amazing."

Agent Graham asked, "May I see your skin where the bones broke through?"

Marilyn sat on the bed and after swinging her legs up onto the bed, raised her gown enough to show red lines on each leg. "Those red lines are fading."

Agent Bourne said, "We're done here."

I was the last to leave the room and I covered her legs and gave her a kiss on the cheek. "Thank you." Before leaving as well.

CHAPTER SIX

I drove into the parking lot of the Greater Kansas City Martial Arts Center for my appointment with Master Yow. It looked to be an old school building that had been converted to its present use. Knowing how my past Judo instructors valued being on time I had allowed myself an extra fifteen minutes as I entered the front entrance and approached a counter with a pretty petite Asian woman dressed in a gi with a brown belt.

I gave her my name and who I had an appointment. After checking her computer she told me to wait for a guide. Soon an Asian male wearing a gi with a black belt arrived to guide me to Master Yow.

He knocked on a door and after receiving some kind of greeting, opened the door for me to enter. I sensed him following me into the room and shutting the door. Sitting on a mat on the floor was an old man with long white hair on his head and face, dressed in a red robe. I bowed deeply until he uttered a sound, which I assumed was a signal to rise.

Master Yow motioned me to sit on a cushion eight feet in front of him, which I did. He looked at me for several minutes without speaking, then clapped his hands and using English asked for tea. After we were served by two female brown belts we were again alone except for the black belt at the door.

"You are a black belt, but it has been years since you trained.

You have a strong healing aura and have many talents. I sense that you are a very powerful woman, how can I help you in your journey?"

"My name is Dr. Angel Pearson-Blake and I received my black belt when I was fifteen. While I was in medical school I taught self-defense Judo, but have received no further formal training. Johns Hopkins Hospital wishes to offer free self-defense courses to its staff and we need instructors. We currently have fifty students wishing to take the class; however, we think the total may reach at least sixty. I personally would like an instructor to advance me beyond the first level."

"You don't wish to teach, but prefer to be a student?"

"I love to teach, but demands upon my time won't allow it. The classes would be held at the hospital where we have arranged to have a large room available. If you agree we will purchase all uniforms and equipment that is needed through your center. The current number of students would require Monday through Friday classes at seven in the evening. If this time is not convenient we can consult for a better time."

"The evening time would conflict with our schedules. Would six in the morning be acceptable?"

"That's acceptable. How many instructors do you anticipate needing for ten plus students?"

"How many students did you have in your classes?"

"Twenty. I did have two brown belts to help me."

"You must have been very persuasive to train such a large group, even with the help of two brown belts."

Master Yow raised his voice slightly. "Yue He, how many would you need for ten plus students?"

"Initially one black belt and three browns. Later, after the student's progress to brown belts, then our brown's can be discontinued."

"Who would you have available to train me? I would be paying that fee myself."

"How high a rank to you wish to advance?"

"My parents are both midlevel black belts. I think a level five would satisfy me."

"Your parents are attorneys at Phelps, Phelps & Woodruff?"

"Yes, I got your card from my father. Is there a problem?"

"No. I owe your parents a great debt. There will be no charge for your training, but you need to come here for your lessons. We'll arrange a time later."

"My husband may wish to advance as well. Will that be a problem? I've personally trained him to what I think is a black belt."

Master Yow looked at me, then at Yue He. "Do you think Ming How is ready for two low rank blacks?"

"Yes, but I would want to watch them."

"So would I. This may become a very interesting class."

After making arrangements for someone from the Center to visit the hospital and inspect the prospective class room, I took my leave and returned to the hospital. I informed Dr. Ellsworth of what had been decided and to expect a visitor from the Center to check out our class room. That finished, I inspected the ER before meeting Jeff for our ride home.

I told Jeff about meeting Master Yow and plans for the self-defense Judo classes, then said, "I also made arrangements for us to continue our Judo training. I hope you don't mind."

"We're taking our classes together? Swell, I like that."

"Maybe not. Our instructor is someone named Ming How and from Master Yow's conversation with his lead man, there's something going on there. In any case, our training is free because of a great debt Master Yow owes my parents."

"That's interesting. It seems our lives continue to follow someone's game plan. I wonder what's next?"

Alice greeted us mentally as we entered the apartment and we hurried to make over her. Her nanny, Grace Simpson, told us nothing unusual had happened today with our daughter. Yesterday, Alice had mentally retrieved a toy that had fallen to the floor. This was not unexpected as Aunt Barbara had warned us she would develop these and other powers.

I mentally asked Alice, *"How have you been today? Have you learned any new things you can do with your mind?"*

"No. I do wish I was beyond wearing diapers. It's so nasty!"

"I know, we've talked about this before. Your body takes time to respond to what your brain tells it to do. Can you talk to Elizabeth when she's in her apartment?"

"Yes, I must be getting stronger because I couldn't do that

before."

"Let us know when you discover something new. Your Aunt Barbara tells us that it's going to happen."

"Aunt Barbara talks to me too. She's like another mother to me as I bask in her love."

"Yes, I feel her love too. I'll tell you her story when you are older."

"Mommy, why are only the females in our generations empowered with our abilities?"

"It's God's plan and we were not informed of what his plans are for us. I assume that I will be informed when the time is right. The same applies to you and Elizabeth."

* * *

Dr. Ellsworth wanted me to be present for the first class each day this first week of the hospitals' self-defense Judo classes. I wore my gi and black belt and met the instructors before the students arrived.

I bowed to the higher rank black belt and introduced myself and why I was present for the first classes this week. Maris Carter was a level six black belt and was assisted by three brown belts. All the students had been issued their uniforms, or gis, and white belts (novice). When the students came into the room, the brown belts showed them the proper way to fasten the belt and to remove their shoes.

Maris stood to the side and observed her twelve students as her browns got them settled and then she introduced me. "Some of you know I'm a black belt. I started training when I was ten and achieved my present rank at fifteen. Hopefully, if you stay with the program you too can achieve the rank of black belt. Regardless, your training will give you confidence that you can protect yourself if the need arises. I'll turn the class over to your instructor now. Give them the respect they deserve."

I walked out of the room, but from the doorway observed her as she and her assistants started the students in the basics. I went to my office and changed back into my normal work attire and began my rounds.

Later that day after work, Jeff and I went to the Center to

begin our Judo classes. We were shown a locker room where we changed into our gis. As we entered our class room I noticed a camera mounted high in one corner. There were no other students and I began to wonder if we were shown the correct room, when a short Asian woman wearing a black belt entered. We both gave her a bow of respect, which she acknowledged.

"I am Ming How and will be your instructor. I want to observe your abilities by watching you spar with each other using your most advanced moves. Please begin."

Jeff and I bowed to each other and then moved apart slowly circling watching for the other to make a move. I moved my right leg out as if to move, but instead attacked Jeff's weak side when he moved to counter what he thought was my first move. Jeff countered my attack and we both tried several more times to gain an advantage.

Ming How said, "Enough! Stand down. You are trained equally to a high level one or a low two. Angel will be my victim, so watch my moves against her."

I cleared my mind as I watched for her to move. She was very fast as she rushed me, much faster than I thought a five foot woman could move. I only had one move open to me as I jumped straight up, did a flip and landed on her back. When we both regained our feet I again gave her a bow.

Ming How said, "That's a level six move. How did you learn it?"

"My mother showed me the basics."

"How many more moves above a level two do you know?"

"Not many. Mother said I should know some moves in case I encounter a higher level opponent."

Ming How looked at me with a slight smile. "I think Master Yow is having a little joke at my expense. That's the first time I've been bested by a lower level opponent and I have learned my lesson. Never assume that they don't know a move that can beat you. Okay, for the purpose of this lesson don't use any moves above a level 2. Now let's try that again."

At the end of the hour plus lesson, both Jeff and I were beat. Even Ming How looked like she had a workout. We showered and dressed and Jeff had me drive home as I was the stronger. After relieving Grace we ordered in delivery Chinese as neither one of us wanted to cook. Jeff threw our gis into the washer while I took care of Alice.

"Mommy, why are you and daddy so tired? You haven't been this way before."

"We took a Judo lesson, the first one in years and we were not in shape. Next time will not be as hard."

"I used the potty today for the first time. Grace started me on pull ups until I'm sure I can make the potty every time."

"That's wonderful honey. Have you done anything else that's new?"

"No. Can I have some of your meal. The last time you had Chinese it smelled wonderful."

"Okay, but not very much. I don't want to make your poop runny."

That night we took turns giving each other massages. Jeff's muscles were so knotted I had to use a little physic healing to get them to loosen up. That night we fell into each other's arms and didn't stir until the alarm sounded the next morning.

The morning TV news featured a piece on the first lady's visit in Independence, Missouri early this afternoon to dedicate a new business owned and managed by women. I commented to Jeff that the Secret Service would be busy today. After arriving at the hospital early so that I could make a showing at the second Judo class, I finished that task and used the remaining quiet time to review my department budget.

I was about to take a lunch break with Lilly and Bob when the ER was flooded with EMTs, Secret Service, and police. I yelled, "I'm in charge here. What's going on?"

The lead agent said, "The First Lady and her two children were involved in a helicopter crash just short of the Missouri River after leaving Kansas City International Airport. Everyone on board was injured. If you are Dr. Angel Pearson-Blake your task is the well-being of the first family. Your staff can handle the other patients as they arrive."

"Lilly, you and Bob take the kids while I check on the First Lady. Doctors get to it on a first come basis."

I called Dr. Ellsworth to get other doctors and staff to help with the rush, then checked on my patient. I touched her arm and found broken bones, pierced left lung, and minor cuts. I started to instruct my nurse to begin dressing the cuts when I realized they were all busy. I yelled, "Dr. Upton come here now."

When I felt her presence at my side I gave her the simple injuries, while I started on the major tasks. But first I had to remove the patient's clothing to make sure there were no other cuts, which the two of us handled with a grimace as thousands of dollars' worth of ruined clothing landed on the floor. I told Dr. Upton what the First Lady's major injuries were and what I was doing first. She was unconscious and heart rate was steady, but her breathing was labored because of the pierced lung.

I first removed the broken rib from her lung, then fused the lung tissue tear. I moved the broken rib back into place and fused the broken ends together. Her broken collar bone was repaired next, then I moved down and repaired her right arm that was broken in two places. Dr. Upton was still working on the cuts when I finished, so I checked her vitals again. Everything was in the normal range. I went to the Secret Service agent and told him the First Lady's injuries were repaired except for some cuts I would take care of later. I recommend that she remain here overnight and I was going to check on the children now.

I told Dr. Upton to remain with her patient until I returned, then headed to the closest child. I asked Lilly, "What's his condition?"

"Stable, major cuts have been bandaged."

I placed my hand on his arm and found he had internal bleeding, broken left leg, and right hand with a dislocated finger. I found the cause of the internal bleeding and repaired it and the broken leg, and fixed the finger. I told Lilly I would return to work on the cuts, then moved to the final child.

She was looking at me with wide eyes when I approached her. I placed my hand on her head. "Where does it hurt honey?"

"I just have a broken right leg. Mommy and Jake were hurt really bad. Are they alright?"

"I just finished with them and they will be fine. Are you a doctor, because your diagnosis was right on the money?"

She grimaced. "It hurts some. Are you going to fix it now?"

I looked at Bob. "Any cuts for me to heal?"

"No, just a few scratches."

"Okay, do you want anything to bite on while I fix your leg?"

"Will it hurt bad?"

"Not for you. I already fixed it. That wasn't bad was it?"

"You're funny, what's your name?"

"Dr. Angel Pearson-Blake. What's your name?"

"Nicole Marie, but I prefer Marie."

"Well, Marie I'm going to put the final touches on your Mommy and Jake and then we are going to put you all together in a room. What kind of snack does your mommy let you have?"

"Strawberry Ice Cream, but only if we are very good."

"I'll ask her later. Hope to see you again. Bye."

I soon healed the cuts of both the First Lady and Jake. I returned to the lead Secret Service agent. "The First Family is healed and ready to be moved to a large hospital room that will hold all three patients. I know you are concerned about security. We have the same type room on any floor of the hospital except the surgery suites, your pick. I do recommend that they spend the night to make sure they are stabilized. The First Lady and Jake are still unconscious, but I expect that to change soon. You think on that while I check on the other patients."

There were six other patients including the two pilots. I started with who appeared to be the worst injured and made my way through all of them in the next hour. Three had only minor injuries and were released, while the other three were admitted. The pilots had the least injuries because they were securely strapped in and the helicopter struck the ground tail first.

I checked back with the lead SS agent, "I got approval for the First Family to stay overnight, but they are scheduled to depart tomorrow morning at nine from KCI. I think the sixth floor will provide us with better security. Give us a room number and we'll check it out."

I called registration and got a room in the new wing. "You have room 640. If it's not satisfactory let us know."

CHAPTER SEVEN

Two hours later I checked on my patients starting with the First Family. There was security at the elevators on the first floor and on the sixth floor. I had them call ahead to room 640 to expect me. When I arrived my ID was checked before I was allowed into the room. Everyone was awake this time as I made the rounds starting with the First Lady, Julia Clark. I checked her chart and touched her wrist getting a direct reading of her condition.

"Mrs. Clark, for your own information I repaired a tear in your right lung caused by a broken rib, which I also repaired. I also repaired a broken collar bone and your right arm that was broken in two places. Jake had a broken left leg, internal bleeding from a bruised pancreas, and a dislocated finger on his right hand. Marie had a broken right leg. All their injuries have been repaired. I've had scans and x-rays prepared so that your doctors can verify the injuries existed, but eventually evidence of the injuries will disappear including your cuts. By the way, only Marie was awake when I made the repairs and she was a very brave little girl. I promised her strawberry ice cream subject to your approval."

"Dr. Angel Pearson-Blake. I assume the Blake is your married name. I didn't believe the reports provided by the Secret Service, but here you are as reported. Marie already told me about her conversation with you as you fixed her leg. She wants to be a doctor now just like you, but unfortunately that's not possible, is it?"

"Just like me, no. However, she can be a doctor and the practice is rewarding for those who enter into it. I have a younger sister who is following in my footsteps as a healer and a daughter who may be more powerful than either of us. My husband is working here at Johns Hopkins as the lead surgeon and is very gifted, but not like my sister, myself, or my daughter."

"About that ice cream, can I get butter pecan."

I smiled at her. "Why not, but you better call down to the kitchen and get an agent to bring it up or it will be melted before it gets to you."

That brought a laugh from everyone in the room as I went to check on Jake, who was fine. Then it was Marie's turn as I held her hand. You check out just fine. Do you want to walk over and get in your mother's bed? I'll make sure you don't fall."

"May I mother?"

"Just for a little while until the ice cream gets here."

Marie scampered out of her bed and was soon with her mother, who put her arm around her daughter. "I assume we all are able to walk if she can do that."

"Yes, but no running or jumping for at least a month. Family walks will do you all good and should be done daily. If there are no questions I'll continue my rounds."

I checked on the others from the crash that were admitted and they all were well enough to be released tomorrow with the First Family. I thought to myself, *well, now that's taken care of maybe I can return to my regular schedule. But first, I'd better check with Janice to see if there's anything else to worry about.*

I pulled out my cell and called Dr. Ellsworth's secretary. "Mary, this is Dr. Pearson-Blake. Does your boss need me for anything? I've been out of touch because of the First Family business."

"Yes, she wants to talk to you as soon as you are free."

"Okay, I'll be right there. Can you have someone bring us coffee? I'm bushed."

I stopped at the ER on my way to the Administrator's office to check on my residents. They were both in the break room, which made it convenient for me. Hanna and Taylor had their heads together talking quietly when I sat at their table.

"Well, doctors that was quite an experience. Something to tell your kids about when you have any. How are you feeling?"

Dr. Upton said, "You are awesome. If I hadn't seen you work I wouldn't have believed it. I'm still jazzed from the experience."

"How about you, Dr. Wilson? Is this the experience you were hoping for when you applied here?"

"How do you handle this excitement time after time. I'd be burned out after a month."

"Don't say that because I need both of you. Take three days off and recharge and I want you back here ready for whatever comes our way."

They both gave me a wan smile as I got up and left the room. I soon arrived at Dr. Ellsworth's office and Mary showed me right in where I took a seat and visibly sank into the chair. Janice smiled at me. "That was a rough few hours. Not only the work, but the pressure from who they were. There's coffee over there, help yourself."

I did as she advised and sat back down and sipped my drink while trying to relax. "Anything else happen while I was busy?"

"The Atomic Energy Agency took their witness and left the hospital. That's one less problem for us."

"How about the mess she left behind?"

"The room she was in is clean of radiation, but the bed and linens had to be destroyed. I'm sending a bill to them to pay for that and for the time she was here."

"Ha. Don't hold your breath. I'm just glad we don't have to worry about someone trying to kill her here again."

"Jeff and I had our first Judo lesson yesterday. We didn't know how out of shape we were until our five foot woman instructor finished with us. I have to admit that we gave her a good workout too."

"Just don't overdo it. We need you both here uninjured. The first two staff Judo classes seem to have gone well, as all I've received is positive feedback."

"The First Family will be leaving in the morning, so that's another stressful problem that we can check off."

"That's not finished yet. The lead Secret Service agent wants you to give a press conference later this morning addressing the family's injuries and possible release date. They leave it up to you if you want to describe their injuries you repaired."

"Do you think I should go into detail or just gloss it over?"

"Angel, you've already described to the press what you're capable of. I'd give them the whole truth and see if they choke on it."

"Where is this news conference going to take place and at what time?"

"In one hour at the conference room where the Judo classes are held. It's already been prepped, so go prepare yourself and good luck."

I called Jeff and told him about the news conference and that I wanted him there for moral support. I then called Mom and Dad so they wouldn't miss their daughter on the National News. I returned to the ER and gathered both residents, who hadn't left yet on their time off, and an ER doctor to show I didn't do all the work by myself. I explained to them the reason I needed them and all three went white-faced in fear of facing the cameras.

"I was thinking of having you two residents tell what happened from your prospective. Is that okay?"

Taylor and Hanna both backed against the wall and Taylor said, "No! No, no, please don't do that. I'm sure I'll stammer or faint in front of the cameras."

"I was just kidding. But, you may have to do that some time in the future, especially if you continue to work with me. I'll carry the ball, you just stand behind me and look competent. Now go look pretty for the cameras and I'll do the same."

At the appointed time we all entered together and stood against the back wall while Dr. Ellsworth took the podium. There was much noise of shutters and flashes of light from the still cameras before she raised her hand and began speaking about the arrival of the First Family into their ER along with other injured personnel from the crash. She then introduced me, "Doctor Angel Pearson-Blake is the head of the ER and Emergency Medicine and was in charge of their care when they arrived."

If anything, there was more camera activity than when Dr. Ellsworth took the podium as I stood there with a smile on my face. When I felt it was time, I held up my hand and began telling what my team did for the patients as they arrived. I explained the injuries to Julia Clark, who I worked on first, and how I repaired each injury. Then I detailed the injuries of both children and how I repaired them. I explained how they were all unconscious when I worked on them, except for Nicole Marie, who was concerned about her mother and brother. I then asked for questions.

One of the three letter networks' reporter asked, "You claim to have healed all their injuries. Does that mean they are ready to leave the hospital?"

"I recommended that they remain overnight to make sure they are stabilized."

Another network reporter asked, "Are you the same Angel Pearson who was a healer by touch when you were a child?"

"Yes, I lost that ability when I was fifteen. In its place I've been given other gifts."

"I have a follow-up question, "Do you have a young sister who is now a healer like you were at that age?"

"Yes, she practices here at this hospital on need. Are there any more questions relating to the First Family? My background has been thoroughly covered in a special interview after the hospital first opened. Please refer to that if you have questions about me. If that's not sufficient, feel free to make an appointment for a follow up."

The only other question was the time of the First Family's release from the hospital and I referred that to the lead agent. I stepped back with a sigh of relief as the agent gave a late morning departure tomorrow. We had already made arrangements for them to fly from the roof of the hospital on several helicopters to KCI, where they would depart to Washington on Air Force Two.

After the news conference ended I told my residents to go ahead and start their time off, but I wanted them back ready to work in three days. They gave me a small smile before disappearing in the crowd of news people. I had just released my ER doctor who I had brought with me, when I felt a tap on my shoulder.

I turned to find three well-known network news commentators with expectant expressions on their faces. I said, "Yes?"

Alan Peterson of XYZ Network said, "We think that there is a great human interest story here on how your ER handled this near disaster with the First Family. We have agreed to share this story with each other and broadcast it at the same time and date on each of our networks. We'll work with you on the content before it's aired if you'll agree to work with us."

"Why limit it to just the major networks? Why not make the live feed available to any network for a reasonable fee."

The big three huddled together for less than a minute then Peterson said, "I don't think that will be a problem, but our lawyers will need to hash it out. We will send you a contract later and arrange a time for the recording. I hope we can get this done because it holds such great promise."

All three shook my hand and departed, excitingly talking to each other. Janice said at my shoulder as we both watched them leave, "They seemed happy and that story will be great PR for the hospital."

"Yes, it will. However, my parents will have to review that contract when it arrives to be sure there are no hidden traps."

Janice said, "Oh well, back to the salt mines. See you later."

Jeff gave me a hug. "Great job honey. What did the big guns want from you?"

"An in-depth interview relating to how our ER handled the injuries of the First Family, to be shared by all the networks and aired at the same time."

"Wow! I don't think that's ever been done before and it's going to have to happen soon for it to be timely."

"Yeah. I'm going to call my parents tonight and ask them to review the contract when it comes. Janice thinks it will be great PR for the hospital."

Three days later I received the contract by special messenger, which I reviewed and made several notations in the margins, then sent it by messenger to my parents. I gave them a call to let them know it was heading their way, before resuming my duties.

That night my parents knocked at my door and we went over my initial concerns and some of their own before we were satisfied with the changes. I said, "Why not add a provision where they advertise for donations to the Elizabeth Foundation to cover expenses for those people Elizabeth healed who can't afford the hospital's charges. We need to increase the fund because of the anticipated increase in her patients because of this broadcast."

They made the changes and faxed the altered contract to the number of the networks' attorneys. Elizabeth had been watching over Alice while we had been concerned with the contract and with that done, my parents wanted to play with their granddaughter. Mother picked up Alice and I touched her arm to enable her to mentally hear Alice.

Alice's mental voice was getting stronger and she surprised mother when she said, *"Grandma, can you hear me?"*

"Oh my goodness, Alice is talking to me!"

"I know. She's been mentally talking to Elizabeth and us and now you. Have Dad come over and touch you and we can have a three-way conversation."

Dad came over with a incredulous expression on his face and touched Mom. *"Grandpa, I can talk to you all now. Momma, it might not be the time to mention me on that program you're going to do. Aunt Barbara advices against it at this time."*

Mother said, *"She talks like an adult. How is that possible at only eighteen months?"*

"Mother, Alice is not a normal child. Remember we're talking to her with our thoughts."

"Grandma, I'm using my potty now and wearing pull-ups. When did you start giving momma something good to eat? Baby food is not nearly as good as what you eat."

"Oh honey, I know. You have to continue with that stuff until your body can accept adult food, maybe another six months. Is that right Angel?"

"Some say two years, but if we gradually give her small portions we can judge how she is tolerating solid food."

"Elizabeth, how am I progressing compared to you?"

"We both learned to walk and cut our teeth at about the same age, but I learned to talk over six months earlier than your mental conversations. Have you tried to vocally speak?"

"Yes, I speak to Grace, but my vocal voice is so weak. I prefer to speak mentally now that we are all connected."

I said, *"Alice, speaking with your vocal voice requires practice to make it stronger. At some point you may be required to communicate with others using your vocal voice and until we are able to hear your mental voice without touching someone else who is prime in the family, your vocal voice is more convenient for us."*

"Okay, how do I sound?"

"Like a fifteen year old in a eighteen month old body. Alice try not to sound like an adult when there are others present who are not aware of your abilities. Use two or three word sentences when you want something. Do you understand?"

"Yes mommy. You want me to act my age with others."

"I'll mentally let you know if it's okay to talk to outsiders."

CHAPTER EIGHT

Nothing changed for a week as I did my normal routine. Jeff's and my Judo classes continued, but our instructor seemed to treat me with extra care. After the class I said, "Ming How, you have no reason to fear me. Why the caution when we spar?"

"Master Yow informed me who you are after the first lesson. I no wish to harm such a powerful person as yourself. It would reflect badly upon me. Bad karma!"

I walked up and hugged her, which caused her to tear up. "Ming How, I'm tougher than I look. I can't learn what I need to know if you hold back. If you become too rough I'll tell you, I promise."

"You sure? Alright, next class prepare to hurt."

On the drive home Jeff snickered. "Next class prepare to hurt! I can't believe you told her to come on full bore."

"She was holding back with me and you were getting better instruction. Remember we have a bet on which of us advances faster."

After arriving home we fussed over our daughter after relieving Grace from her nanny duties. We explained to Alice that we needed to take a shower and would return shortly as we placed her in a safe room. Fifteen minutes later we brought her with us as Jeff and I traded giving each other a massage.

"Mommy, daddy really likes what you are doing to him. Your

Judo class seems to have stressed many muscle groups in both your bodies. Is he going to rub your muscles like you're doing to him now?"

"He'd better or he won't get any more from me."

"I see. You each help the other achieve relief from sore muscles. I'm sorry I can't be of any help at this time. My hands are too small and weak to be of any use. Mommy, I want to learn to read. Can you help me?"

"I think I can. I'll have to get some beginning books, but I think many of them would be too elementary for 'you. Tomorrow we'll go to a bookstore together and pick some out."

Soon I finished with Jeff and we traded places. It wasn't long before his magic fingers elicited a moan of relief from me. "Mommy, is that a good feeling or pain?"

"It's a very good feeling."

"Good. Daddy, keep doing that. I think she likes it."

The next day a revised contract for the news program arrived by messenger. They had accepted all my changes, so I signed it, made two copies and returned it by messenger. I took one of the copies to Janice for her information, then returned to my duties.

Two days later I received a telephone call from Alan Peterson, the lead news commentator for XYZ Network. "Dr. Pearson-Blake, we are going to tape the show at six p.m., Wednesday of next week, at the XYZ affiliate station on South Broadway in Kansas City. You should be there by five p.m. for makeup and introduction to the other commentators. A film crew will be at the hospital later this week to take background shots of Johns Hopkins Hospital and the ER where the First Family arrived. Please prepare a one minute script you want to use for the Elizabeth Foundation commercial you want us to run."

"You plan on taping the commercial at the time I'm there for the program? You want me wearing a lab coat or a suit?"

"Bring both and we will decide when you get here."

"Are you going to have anyone else from the hospital on the program, such as the administrator?"

"You have a point. Tell Dr. Ellsworth to come as well. We can ask her for background information on you."

"Very well. I'll inform everyone to expect the film crew and Dr. Ellsworth that she is invited to the taping as a participant."

I used my cell to call mother and told her of the taping date next week and asked her to help me prepare a script for the Elizabeth Foundation commercial.

"How long can the commercial be?"

"One minute or less and I'll be the one talking. You might give me some hints on my on-screen demeanor."

"Okay, your father and I will get back to you later. Now, take a deep breath and let it out slowly. This is nothing you haven't done before, so put it behind you. Remember, you are the only one with her clothes on. Everyone else is naked."

"I'm not sure that's the vision I want in my mind when I'm speaking. I might start laughing and how would I explain that?"

"Angel, you know that was only a metaphor."

"I know. I was trying to put a little humor into our conversation. Mother you are so uptight. I'm going to have to expose you to more humor in your life before you ruin poor Elizabeth."

"Oh poo! I certainly didn't ruin you. Why did you say that? Did Elizabeth complain about me?"

"No, you couldn't ruin her if you tried. This just proves my point. You are so defensive. Go with the flow, smile, tell a joke. Ask father for a good joke if you can't think of one. Tell the joke to Alice tonight and see how she responds. I so want her to have a sense of humor."

After ending the call I started my rounds at the ER. Everyone was busy with walk-ins, people mostly without health insurance and/or a primary doctor. I observed everyone for a time and then moved on until I caught Lilly's attention and motioned for her to join me.

"How are my residents doing since they got back from their time off?"

"The way they're acting they both got lucky. Whatever was bothering them is gone now."

"Great! I was thinking I've been working them too hard. Tell everyone that at shift's end to meet me in my office."

I made my way to Dr. Ellsworth's office where I informed her that she and I were invited as participants in next week's taping of the news program. We discussed several things that we wanted to talk about on the program.

I asked, "Do you think President Smithson has any interest in being part of this program?"

"No, but he is taking a keen interest in how we are conducting ourselves and how it reflects upon Johns Hopkins reputation. So far he is very happy with the way things are going."

* * *

The day of the taping of the news program arrived and Jeff and I met Dr. Ellsworth at the studio. While Janice and I were touched up for the camera, Jeff tried to get my mind off the interview and was telling me his mother's reaction to Alice's abilities.

I raised my eyebrow at him through the mirror. "Jeff really, she raised you and your sisters. I don't think there's anything that would surprise her after that experience."

"We'll see when she has her first experience with Alice inside her head. I know you've told Alice not to do that, but it's a really hard temptation for her. After all, she's not even two yet."

Time seemed to fly and suddenly Janice and I were sitting together facing the lead commentators from the three major networks. Alan Peterson from the XYZ Network gave a quick background leading up to the three networks combining their efforts to show how Johns Hopkins Hospital of Kansas City treated the First Family after they were injured when their helicopter crashed after leaving KCI.

Peterson then started asking questions by having the hospital administer, Dr. Janice Ellsworth, describe my history with Johns Hopkins from medical school, residency, then as head of Emergency Medicine and Unconventional Medicine at this hospital.

"Dr. Ellsworth it seems rather unusual for a doctor to go from a resident to a Department Head. To your knowledge has that ever happened before?"

"It has never happened at Johns Hopkins or any other hospital to my knowledge. However, no one else has her abilities."

"Dr. Angel Pearson-Blake, according to what she has said in past interviews, has the ability to diagnose illness or injuries by touch. At the press conference held after treating the First Family, she said she repaired broken bones, internal bleeding from a bruised pancreas, a torn lung caused by a broken rib, and associated cuts. She did all this without cutting into the body and when finished she caused even the external cuts to disappear. Based upon this alone, Dr. Pearson-Blake is a miracle worker."

Jerry Walker from KRK network asked, "Dr. Pearson-Blake when you were about ten years of age you had the ability to heal by touch. What changed?"

"God took away that gift and gave me another when I was fifteen. I was told to seek medical training."

"You did undergraduate work at Missouri University starting at age fifteen, then three years later began medical school at Johns Hopkins. You graduated as your class' Valedictorian in three and half years, something no one else has ever done before at that school. According to the school's records you didn't just study. You also hold a black belt in Judo and started a class at the urging of the school. Apparently, some kind of conflict arose where your class was attacked by several men who were soundly defeated and carted off to jail without any injuries to the class. Based upon how fast you finished your schooling, you must be very smart."

"I have genus IQ of 156 and a eidetic memory. That means I can remember anything I read, see, or hear."

Mary Sullivan of CCA Network said, "You said you were head of Emergency Medicine and Unconventional Medicine. What's unconventional medicine?"

"That's what I did with the First Family. Normally, their injuries would have been handled by doctors doing conventional medicine that would have resulted in a much longer convalescent period and some scarring. The Secret Service convinced me that for security reasons I should use my gifts on them. If for any reason I'm unable to use my gifts, then my sister, Elizabeth Pearson, is a healer by touch. Her services are usually used only when there is no other option. At this time she heals about forty patients every month, but that may change after this broadcast."

"What you are saying is that Johns Hopkins has three levels of care for its patients. What I would call normal care is conventional medicine, unconventional medicine is handled by you for those patients too risky for conventional medicine, and the last is for those too hopeless for the other two conventions. Your sister,

Elizabeth Pearson, is your replacement as a healer by touch. I'm curious how all this came about. Do you have any understanding why this occurred?"

I looked at Mary Sullivan a moment before smiling. "Does anyone understand the reasons God does things? It did give me the opportunity for a life outside of healing by touch, and I now have a child who is the love of my life. Perhaps Elizabeth will be given the same opportunity as I was."

The three network commentators continued to take turns asking about how the hospital's ER worked compared to others in the metro area, how I was tagged to do unconventional surgery when I was not part of the surgical staff, and how many patients I handle in a month. Eventually they ran out of questions and the news program ended.

They then shot the commercial for donations to the Elizabeth Foundation. I smiled at the camera, which according to mother, could make anyone do as I asked. I then explained how the foundation worked, paying the hospital expenses of indigent patients when they came to be cured of their terminal illness. I explained how much the foundation had paid since Elizabeth started her healing at the hospital and how donations were needed for her to continue her work to all who sought her healing."

Satisfied that I had done the best I could, I met with Jeff and Janice and asked them if they thought the program went well? Janice said, "The part we saw here looked real good. We'll have to see how it's going to be put together. Can I watch it with you when the program is broadcast? I get anxious when I'm on TV and I'd prefer friends were with me."

I agreed and Jeff and I left to drive home. On the way, Jeff said, "Angel, I don't know if the camera caught it, but you glowed. There was a purple haze around you throughout the taping. You need to smile more the next time you do one of these broadcasts. I swear your smile could melt the camera. Remember that smile captured me."

"I've heard from several people now about that purple glow or aura of mine. I wonder what that means."

Three days later the networks were advertising that a special news program would preempt regular programming on Sunday evening at nine, and that it would be an in-depth review of how the

First Family's injuries were taken care of after their helicopter crash. The advertisement prominently showed me being interviewed.

I used my cell to call Janice and told her to be at my apartment by eight on Sunday so that she could meet Alice. Sunday afternoon before Janice was due to arrive, I told Alice, "My supervisor from the hospital is coming to view the airing of the news program we've been talking about. You may address her as Janice if you feel she is a friend, or Dr. Ellsworth if you want to be formal. You may talk to her mentally if it's possible, or by your voice. I like her and she's been a good friend to me."

"So I don't have to act my age with her?"

"That's right. She already knows about your ability to converse mentally. I can touch her if that would make the mental conversation possible."

"Mommy, I'll let you know if I need your help."

At the appointed time Janice arrived and while carrying Alice I let her inside. Alice was quite a handful, but I managed to make the introductions without dropping her. Janice smiled at my daughter and when she held out arms to Janice, she gladly took her from me and sat in a chair with Alice on her lap.

"Janice, this is Alice speaking to you. Can you hear me?"

"Yes! Angel told me you were starting to mentally talk to your family, but I had no idea you were able to talk to me."

"You are the first outsider I've tried to talk to. I can read your surface thoughts. Try to block me from doing that. Yes, that did it."

Alice leaned up against Janice and gave her a big smile. Janice smiled in return and said, "Angel, she's just precious and that smile of hers just draws me to her."

"Does her smile remind you of my smile?"

"Why yes, it does. Hers has a stronger draw though."

"She's more powerful than me. So far that makes three powers she has demonstrated. I wonder what's next."

CHAPTER NINE

Just before the broadcast my parents and Elizabeth came from their adjoining condo to watch the program with us. Elizabeth immediately took charge of Alice and they sat on the floor while the adults used the available chairs. I asked anyone if they wanted drinks or popcorn, and after fulfilling their wishes I sat next to Jeff who put his arm around me.

Alan Peterson from the XYZ Network started off by giving the audience a little background of the Johns Hopkins Hospital of Kansas City. They used a city map to show the location of the hospital and the crash site and the time it took for the Secret Service and the EMTs to get to the crash site. The Secret Service had already vetted the hospital in case an emergency occurred and everyone headed toward Johns Hopkins.

They showed the hospital's ER in operation, which was usually busy 24/7. They interviewed members of my ER staff who described how the patients arrived without warning and how I had immediately called for more doctors and assigned them to stabilize the children and the others injured while I started working on Julia Clark, the First Lady.

They cut to my press conference after I treated members of the First Family, where I described the injuries I found and repaired and their current condition. Peterson's face returned to the screen. "It became apparent that Dr. Angel Pearson-Blake's abilities far surpassed medical treatment available elsewhere and we did an in-depth interview with her which follows."

I was wondering if the purple aura could be seen by the camera, but I didn't see anything so I concentrated on our performances on camera. When Janice finished speaking I complimented her on how well she did, then watched as my turn came. As I talked I realized that I started to glow and I said, "Whoa! What's going on with the glow around me?"

Jeff said, "We told you about the glow. Apparently, when you concentrate there is a by-product produced, as in you glow."

As we watched the program my aura turned from a light to a dark purple, until finally I said, "How can other people not see that?"

Janice said, "They probably do. We'll know after the show when people start to call in."

At the end of the program my face appeared on the screen and I used my special smile to get their attention as I began talking about the Elizabeth Foundation and asking for donations. When the commercial finished I asked, "Do you think that was good enough to get the donations we need?"

Mother said, "Angel, that smile did it. You used the special one that time and I think you are going to be surprised at the result."

Alice said, "Momma, I felt the effects of that smile too. When you smiled at me before, all I felt was love. That smile gave me a feeling of longing, that I should do something to please you."

"Alice, you have the same smile, only much stronger. Try not to use that smile unless you really need to. Elizabeth, do you have that smile too?"

Mother gave a short laugh. "Are you kidding me? I had to put rules on when she could use it. Her nanny complained that when she didn't want to do something or wanted something really bad she would flash her smile and get her way. She's got a stronger smile than you, but maybe not as strong as Alice."

I shook my head in wonder. "I think they are both stronger than me in many ways. Elizabeth and I are tasked to monitor and guide Alice as she comes into her powers. When is your mother, her namesake, coming to visit? We need your mother to establish a relationship with my daughter. Grandmothers in our family have traditionally had great influence over the children they love."

Jeff said, "Her Grandmother Sandra is closer and can spend more time with her."

"You have a point. Let's double team Alice with both her grandmas."

Jeff's cell tone sounded, then looking at who was calling he said, "It's mother."

I rolled my eyes. "Tell her we need to get together."

Alice seemed to be concentrating on the phone conversation, so I picked her up and asked if she wanted some ice cream. That brought her attention back to something she really loved. "Mommy, are you trying to manage me?"

"Of course. That's a mother's duty. Do you want chocolate, vanilla, or strawberry?"

That night after Alice was put to bed and asleep I asked about his conversation with his mother. "She called to congratulate you on the TV show and asked if that purple glow was really coming from you and not something wrong with the TV. I told her it was all you and that it happens when you concentrate. When I told her we needed to talk, she said how about tomorrow at the hospital for lunch."

"That's good. How much does she know about Alice's powers?"

"Only that she's very smart and powerful for her age."

"Oh, Jeff. I didn't want her to be fearful of her when she hears what she can do."

"Angel, you know my mother better than that. She raised two daughters besides me and fear is unknown to her."

The next day Jeff and his mother, Sandra, collected me in my office and we went to the dining area. Sandra and I selected salads while Jeff tried the taco special. Seated, I started to discuss Alice, but was interrupted by several well wishers who had seen the TV program last night. Eventually, I told Sandra of Alice's gifts that we were aware of at this point and what we expected in the future.

"Jeff and I want Alice's grandmothers to offer support and guidance. Tell her stories of the family's history, the strife and conflict that they survived, and how the angels became part of our family. Elizabeth told me that her namesake, Grandmother Elizabeth Pearson, helped her understand her history from

Grandmother Pearson's viewpoint. Alice has three living grandmothers experiences that she can draw upon. Will you help?"

"How can I?"

"How about once a week you take the place of her nanny. You pick the day. If a whole day is more than your schedule allows, a half day will be fine."

Sandra pulled her calendar out of her purse and then said, "Tuesdays are fine beginning next week. I can change any conflicts after that. How about Grandmother Alice, when can she come?"

"When she comes it will be for more than a day. Coffeyville is too far to commute. When she gets here why don't you both overwhelm her with stories? My mother and Elizabeth will have their turn as well."

"Does your daughter know you are making plans about her?"

"Of course. However, she knows we all love her and she gets to bask in all your love and attention."

Two days later Alice asked, "Mommy, I have two names - Alice and April. I know April was Granddad's mother, but nothing other than that."

"When my father was ten, he and April were involved in an automobile wreck that killed his mother. Your granddad was saved by Olivia, his guardian angel. The family has been protected by Olivia ever since."

"So we have two angels looking out for us, Barbara and Olivia. Does everyone have angels protecting them?"

"I don't really know, but ours are proactive in their protection. Olivia protects us from mortal danger and Barbara offers us love and delivers messages from God. Barbara, when she was alive, was Grandma Jenn's older sister. She died in an automobile accident shortly after becoming engaged to marry Grandpa Jack. I think it was her love for Jack and her sister that brought her back as an angel."

"Mama, it seems to me that our family is very unusual. You and Elizabeth are sisters and you are both healers. According to you and Elizabeth, I have powers neither of you have or mine are stronger. It seems God is moving us forward to an unknown goal."

"That's what Elizabeth and I think as well. If you think of anything, let us know."

The following week mother's parents came for a visit from Coffeyville, Kansas, arriving early Friday evening. They hadn't seen Alice in at least six months, so they were surprised and delighted in the changes they found. I had briefed them about her current abilities when I phoned them requesting they visit, so they were not surprised when Alice started to mentally converse with them.

Later, after everyone was settled I ordered Chinese delivery and we talked about what's been happening in the family. Alice seemed to be paying close attention to what was being said about her cousins and other extended relations. After eating dinner we continued talking about our family until it was time for Alice to go to bed.

When I returned to the others, Grandmother Alice asked, "What's the plan?"

"I want Alice to really get to know her grandmothers and their history relating to how the angels became attached to our family. Alice is particularly interested in Barbara since she has talked to her. I gave her a brief outline on what happened, but she needs to know the emotional turmoil the family experienced during this time, especially you as her parents. Mother and dad need to tell their own story to Alice."

"Tell me again why you think we need to do this?"

"Alice is coming into powers that we can't control. I want her to understand the emotional toil her actions might unleash and that she needs to think through any of her actions before she makes them."

"She is so small. Do you really think she will understand what we are trying to do?"

"We can only hope that what we do will be enough to prepare her for what is to come."

CHAPTER TEN

Four years have passed which have brought changes in the family. Alice, now six, is taking college level courses on the computer and no longer uses the keyboard. She operates the computer with her mind and seems to soak up knowledge like a sponge. In addition to operating the computer, she uses her mind to move objects effortlessly. I can now converse mentally with her from the hospital and we don't yet know what her limits are.

Elizabeth is fifteen and still has her ability to heal by touch. Barbara hasn't said anything that would indicate that this will change, but I wasn't given any warning when it happened to me at this age.

My own powers seem to have stabilized and I have concentrated on making them stronger. The only thing new has been my ability to see a person's aura and tell from its color if they are healthy. The depth of color reflects how healthy they are.

Jeff's surgical ability has garnered notice and demand in the Midwest. In addition, demands on my time for unconventional medical treatment has increased to almost fifty percent. I've had to make adjustments in my other duties to meet these demands. To meet all my obligations I was now considering setting limits on my various tasks.

While our family was eating dinner I asked Jeff for his thoughts on how I should adjust my work schedule. Jeff put down his fork and gazed at me with concern. "Honey, this is going to be difficult for you. You are being pulled three ways, supervising Elizabeth's healing operation, supervising and sometimes working in the ER, and finally working in the unconventional medicine department. That's not counting helping out in the surgical department on call. To do all this you're going to have to set limits for each with enough margin to cover emergencies."

Alice said, "Mommy, I can help you with Elizabeth by determining the truly hopeless from the applicants for her healing and I might be able to help you in your work in unconventional medicine."

Jeff and I looked at Alice in surprise, but then after consideration I asked, "Alice, how do you plan on selecting the true hopeless from the applicants?"

"I can sense illness similar to your ability to diagnose and I can read their minds if they are attempting to mislead us about their terminal illness."

"We usually have twenty applicants each day. I'll take you with me and we'll see how you do and how much time you save for us."

The next day Alice sat with me as we interviewed the applicants and at her mental signal I ended the interview. When we were alone, I discussed the applicant with Alice. That first day we eliminated three applicants based upon fraud discovered in their thoughts. The remainder were approved by what we both saw with our senses.

When we finished I compared my old time with this review and found we saved about two hours. What was telling for me was the depth of Alice's abilities. I thought, *how am I going to use her abilities when she's only six. Maybe there's a way if...*

The next day, Lilly and Alice conducted the interviews while I observed. Lilly didn't mind covering for me and she and Alice were friends. They were in the first interview less than five minutes when Alice gave Lilly the signal to end the interview. When we were alone, Alice said, "That person was not sick and was trying to get information for a newspaper article."

I started to get angry, when Alice said, "Don't worry mommy. I planted a thought in his mind that he was doing a very bad thing and to not do anything like that again."

I took a deep breath. "Do you think that thought will stick?"

"Yes mommy. I put it in deep."

Lilly looked at me and shuddered before reluctantly saying, "Okay, who's next?"

I said, "Wait a minute. Alice, I approve of what you did to that imposter, but in the future before you mess with other peoples' minds I want to know what you intend to do and try to understand if there are going to be any unintended consequences."

"What does that mean?"

"It means that something else may happen that you didn't intend or foresee."

"Oh. If you can't foresee it happening, how can you make a judgment about it?"

"Usually you can't, but if you take actions that can be reversed, then when it happens you have an option to consider."

"Yes mommy. I can reverse what I did to him if its needed, and I'll check with you or Lilly before I do something like that again."

"Okay, let's continue with the applicants."

Alice and Lilly were able to free up at least three hours every day that I formerly used to interview applicants for Elizabeth's healing efforts. I still wanted to be present when Elizabeth did her healing, but she was approaching the age where I would no longer be needed. However, I thought she needed to be at least sixteen before she did it alone. When I did leave her side I would have to carefully consider who would replace me, like Lilly with Alice.

I still needed to reduce my work load and considered several possibilities before I settled on one. I found my possible help in the ER break room. I sat at their table and they looked at me in surprise as they gave me a uncertain smile. "Doctors, I have a proposition for you. How would one or both of you like to spend part of your residency in my unconventional medicine department?"

Doctors Taylor Upton and Hanna Wilson gave me a surprised look, then Hanna asked, "What would are duties be? We certainly can't learn how to do what you do."

"I'm trying to reduce my workload, so you would assist me in preparing patients for treatment, do the paperwork associated with that treatment, and help me by supervising the patients' recovery after treatment."

"That sounds like work for only one of us. Do you want us to take turns because this will take us away from our training in ER."

"I know this seems like a job for a nurse, but I haven't the time to train them. I would like both of you to work up a program, then train your replacements. You can do it by shifting back and forth every other week or however you want to work it. Think of it as training in administration and you'll certainly earn a lot of goodwill from me. During the time you do this you'll be working an eight hour shift."

The two residents looked at each other and smiled. Hanna said, "We'll do it. When do we start?"

"Eight a.m. tomorrow. Meet me in my office and I'll get you started."

* * *

Five years later Elizabeth, now twenty, still had her healing powers and is now in charge of her department. Alice, at eleven, was still growing stronger in her abilities. I seemed to have peaked in my powers, but I'm confident in my abilities and have developed a working strategy that allows me to comfortably split my time between unconventional medicine, and the ER.

I now supervise three new residents in ER after my former residents took their boards and became doctors. Dr. Hanna Wilson accepted a position at this hospital in the ER, while Dr. Taylor Upton took a position near Dallas, Texas. Dr. Wilson seemed fascinated by her experiences while working under my supervision and wanted to remain here.

I decided to place the three residents under her direct supervision, while I maintained a close watch on how she performed. The residents were all from the Baltimore Johns Hopkins Hospital and were top performers. Jacob Eiberger was slightly over six foot tall, a red-headed muscular man from Lawrence, Kansas. Sharon Lierz was a petite five foot, four inch woman with raven black hair and olive skin, from Chicago, Illinois. Rachel Scott was an attractive blond five-foot, eight-inch woman from Los Angeles, California.

When I interviewed the residents individually, I had a feeling that Jacob was going to be a problem with the woman. He seemed to have an easy familiarity with the opposite sex, even while I was interviewing him. I decided to try a little proactive guidance.

"Dr. Eiberger I seem to sense that you think women were placed here to solely satisfy your needs. Am I wrong?"

Eiberger's face stilled in surprise, then he looked at me intently as if trying to gauge my intention. Then apparently thinking he knew what I was after said, "I like women and know how to satisfy their needs."

"I'm sure you have had success in the past, but while you are here I don't want you trying your wiles on your fellow residents. If I feel any discord between the three of you I will take action to remove you from the mix. Do you understand me?"

"Yes. Am I free to try my luck with the remainder of the female staff?"

"They should be smart enough to fend you off; however, if you cause problems I'll have to revisit this conversation. I think you would be wise to hunt outside the hospital."

When I gave Dr. Wilson the responsibility for training the three residents I told her of my conversation with Dr. Eiberger about his hunting habits with the opposite sex, and my warning to keep away from hospital personnel.

She responded in disbelief. "What does he think he is, a gift to women?"

"He thinks he is and with that kind of confidence, he apparently is quite successful. Watch him because I'm sure he'll make a run at you, and warn Sharon and Rachel. If they look like they're in trouble, give them more work and let me know."

Two weeks later Dr. Wilson knocked on my door and sat down glum faced. "That idiot Eiberger doesn't seem to understand what no means. I think he needs supervision by a male doctor."

"He's hitting on you and doesn't quit when you say, 'I'm not interested'. How about the female residents? Is he after them too?"

"No. I think they are afraid of him after seeing how hard he is pursuing me."

"Okay. Tell him to report to me and follow him in shortly after he arrives here. Bring in Dr. Bellows with you. I think it would be safer to have a male witness when we do this."

When Dr. Eiberger knocked I asked him to take a seat for a

few minutes until others I invited arrive. Soon Dr. Wilson and Bellows joined us and took seats. I gazed at Eiberger until he started to fidget with nerves.

"Dr. Eiberger do you remember our conversation when you first arrived here? Well, your skirt-chasing has resulted in a problem, just as I warned you about. Dr. Wilson informs me that you won't take no for a answer, even after repeated attempts on your part have failed. Do you have a mental problem that precludes you from accepting that response?"

"She led me on making me think she wanted me, then she says no when she really wants me."

"Dr. Wilson is he correct, did you invite his attentions?"

"No, he gives me the creeps. All he's interested in is a conquest. He brags about women he has satisfied, and how I didn't know what I was missing."

"Dr. Bellows, what have you heard about Dr. Eiberger?"

"I have heard his brags about his female conquests and how they were put on this earth for men to use. He even said that you had the hots for him. He disgusts me."

"Dr. Eiberger I don't think you are the type of resident we are looking for. You can resign or wait for Dr. Ellsworth to agree with me and kick you out of the program. I'll wait for the end of the day for your response."

Eiberger face was red with rage as he shouted. "I quit! You've got it in for me for some reason."

"Very well. Please sign this form and we'll be done with each other."

He stomped over to my desk and glared at me before signing the resignation form, then turned and glared at Dr. Wilson and Bellows before leaving and slamming the door shut. I frowned in disgust. "I should have told him he was unacceptable when I first learned his character during the interview, but I didn't think he was this bad."

Dr. Bellows said, "You couldn't support your findings until now. He has no basis for coming back at you now."

"I better get your testimony now while it's fresh. Dictate it to my assistant and sign it for our files. I'll notify Dr. Ellsworth of his resignation and why. This guy really leaves a bad taste in my mouth. I'm glad I've got a good man to go home to tonight.

CHAPTER ELEVEN

I was in the ER closing a nasty gash in a teenage girl's lower left leg caused by an automobile crash, when I received a mind message from Alice. *Mom, I think you want to review this patient yourself. Do you have some time to check it out real soon?*

I'll be there in a few minutes, as I'm about done here.

Less than fifteen minutes later I noted two black-suited men outside April's review room. Lilly smiled at me as I entered and then leaned her head toward the applicant sitting by herself across from their desk. She was the former First Lady Julia Clark, who appeared very uncomfortable as she looked at me.

I stepped forward with my hand out to her. "Mrs. Clark it's good to see you again. What can I do for you?"

She stood and took my hand in both hers. "I want you to check me out and tell me if you can fix my problem."

"Please take a seat while I consult with my daughter."

"Alice, what do you sense?"

"Mrs. Clark has the start of ovarian and breast cancer. Lilly, quick get her something to throw up in!"

Lilly put the trash basket in her hands just as she upchucked. I wet some paper towels and placed them on her forehead as she continued to heave. After Lilly and I cleaned her up and removed the smelly container, I asked. "Are you ready to continue?"

"Yes please. Is there anything you can do for me to remove

the cancer?"

"Does your family know you're here?"

"No. I swore my doctor to secrecy and came here hoping you can cure me, much like you did before."

"I may be able to remove the cancer, but it's something I haven't tried before. Alice does your talent extend to killing cancer cells?"

"I think so. Maybe if we work together we can locate and kill them."

Mrs. Clark looked between the two of us in confusion. "You said she's your daughter and apparently she has gifts higher than your own, but she looks so young for this kind of responsibility. Alice, how old are you?"

"I'm eleven, but don't try to compare me with your daughter at that age. Think of me as a short Angel. Mom and I can converse mentally and I have talents she doesn't have. Together, we can do about anything except raise the dead."

"I'll arrange a surgery space while Alice finishes her interviews. How do you feel? Can you walk with me to the elevators, or I can get you a wheel-chair?"

"I'm fine now, but my shadows outside will have to be informed about what we are planning."

"Okay, let's get to it. I've got other things to do today as well."

After the Secret Service agents were informed of our plans and the expected time frame of the treatment, the senior agent started calling his people while we walked toward the elevators. I called Dr. Ellsworth while in the elevator and reported what I was planning. It wasn't long before we were in Dr. Jacob Holmes' office. As Chief of Surgery he arranged a suite for us to use.

Dr. Ellsworth soon arrived and consulted with Dr. Holmes and me about the use of Alice in this treatment. I told them, "Think of her as an observer, since she won't touch the patient. They could record the treatment if that would make them feel better. While we are waiting for Alice to finish downstairs we should document the cancer by taking scans."

They agreed and Mrs. Clark was taken off for that purpose with the agents in tow. I returned to the ER and checked with Dr. Wilson. When Wilson saw me enter the ER she headed in my direction. I asked, "How are our residents adjusting?"

Hanna grinned. "They are relieved that the asshole is gone and think you are a god for the way you handled him. I believe we have a couple of good ones here. They take instructions well and show a willingness to use their brains."

"Good! Alice and I are going to be working on Mrs. Clark, the former First Lady. I'll try to get back here ASAP, but it may be later than I think. Any problems that develop will have to be handled by the senior doctor. Wish me luck."

I returned to the surgery floor and met Jeff in the hallway. "Hey honey I hear you're going to be working on a VIP."

I smiled as I gave him a hug and a kiss. "Yeah, Alice is going to help me find all the cancer tissue. If you have time you should watch, although it's all going to be mental work."

"This is the first time that you've worked together like this. This may be groundbreaking for everyone."

"That's what Dr. Holmes said too. I just hope we don't screw up and miss anything."

He pulled me to him in a hug. "Angel, it's not in you to do anything but your very best. I'm not worried a bit. How about Alice, is she confident?"

"She's the one that suggested we do it together. The little dickens has enough confidence for the both of us. I really think we can do this."

Lilly escorted Alice to the surgery floor and left her with me before returning to the ER. While we were waiting for Mrs. Clark to return from her testing, I mentally asked Alice, *how are you planning on instructing me where the cancer cells are located?*

I will become part of your mind, guiding your thoughts to the proper location. Maybe I can become you while you are searching. This is new to me too; we'll just have to see how we can make it work.

Alice, I'm afraid that this may mentally change both of us. How sure are you?

Barbara said we could do it!

I took a deep breath and hugged Alice. "Let's go back to Dr. Holmes' office and talk to Dr. Ellsworth."

Dr. Ellsworth was sitting at Dr. Holmes' desk making a phone call when we entered. We sat and waited until she finished before asking, "Have you heard how much longer it's going to be before they finish testing?"

"They should be here shortly. Alice, you look more like your mother and Elizabeth every time I see you."

"Thank you Dr. Ellsworth. Are your allergies giving you a problem again? You seem a little congested."

"I know. I guess it's something I just have to live with."

"Maybe not. When we have more time I'll think on it. It's possible that there is a solution."

Dr. Ellsworth gave me a sharp look, then shrugged her shoulders. "Why not. You might give the common cold some thought too."

Mrs. Clark arrived and we took her to the surgery suite where we prepared her for the treatment. Once she was on the table I said, "Julia, I'm not giving you any anesthetic since we aren't going to do any cutting; however, if you have any discomfort, be sure to let us know. Before we start this treatment do you have anything to say?"

"May God guide you."

Alice stood beside me as I placed my hand on Julia's hip and mentally felt my way toward her cancer. I could feel Alice's presence, as if she was looking over my shoulder, then it was as if we were one entity. The cancer cells seemed to glow in my mind as I willed them out of existence as I went deeper looking for more cancer cells. When I was sure there was no more cancer in her ovaries, we did an overview of Julia's body looking for more cancer cells. All we found were in her left breast, which we concentrated on until no more cancer cells were found. We then did a scan of Julia's body, starting at her head and continued down to her feet without finding any cancer or other medical problem.

Alice left my mind and we both breathed deeply in relief and satisfaction. I then hugged Alice and looking with concern into her eyes, asked. "Do you feel okay, no headache or stress?"

"I'm fine, Mom. We merged minds without any difficulty at all. Maybe it helped that you were my mother. How about you, any problems?"

"No, none at all. I could feel your presence, then we were as one. We used each other's talents to get the job done."

Suddenly realizing I had other concerns I leaned over my patient. "Julia, how do you feel?"

"I feel wonderful. Do you think you got it all?"

"Yes, we did a final mental scan and couldn't find anything, but we want to do another machine scan to compare with the first to double check how well we did. When that's done and reviewed I'll talk to you again. I'm pretty sure you can leave the hospital later today."

The nurses transferred Mrs. Clark to a wheel-chair and took her away for more scans. I looked around the empty surgery room. "Let's go back to Dr. Holmes' office and see who's there."

I found the office almost full of doctors with expectant faces. Doctors Ellsworth, Holmes, and Jeff were there and they all smiled when I gave them a thumbs up. "Alice and I do good work together. Mrs. Clark is taking her after-treatment scans and I'm sure they will come back clean."

Jeff said, "Alice, how did it feel working with your mother on such a difficult task?"

"It was new for both of us, but since I knew it could be done I didn't have any fear as I entered Mom's consciousness. We merged and acted as one finding and eliminating cancer cells. When we finished, I just returned to my body without any problems."

"What did you mean when you said you knew it could be done?"

I said, "Barbara told her it would work. When Alice told me that, I had no more qualms about it working."

Dr. Ellsworth said, "Doctors this is a momentous occasion. I just wish it was one where other doctors could be trained to use it. Angel, you and Alice working together can do miracles, but there is a limit to how many patients you can help. Elizabeth can fill a large gap, but even with you three working full time you will only help a small percentage of those in need."

Dr. Holmes said, "This hospital is going to be a Mecca for people who need treatment. Many will come who don't need help from Elizabeth, Angel, or Alice, but because of the reputation of this hospital's care of patients. I think we need to consider adding another wing soon."

Dr. Ellsworth turned to me. "Angel, was this part of what you foresaw when you were making plans for a hospital in Kansas City?"

"Not in my wildest dreams. Barbara has guided my decisions

without disclosing what the long-term goals were. She said future goals are influenced by things that occur by chance; for example Mrs. Clark, a very big VIP who once used our facility, and because of that came back with a problem that Alice and I were just now able to help her with. Is this fate or a guiding hand? I just thought we would be a big draw for a hospital in the Midwest. Now we will probably be known world-wide."

Dr. Ellsworth just looked at me in wonder for a moment. "I'm going to have to call President Smithson and bring him up to date on what just happened here and ask for advice on how to proceed. In the meantime you better prepare a new allocation of your time based upon what seems likely will occur when news gets out on what you are capable of."

Mrs. Clark was returned to my office when the tests were completed. She and Alice were visiting while I reviewed the findings and compared the before and after scans for any abnormalities. Satisfied with my findings, I asked Julia, "How old are your children now?"

"Jake is sixteen and Marie is fourteen. Marie still wants to be a doctor, but I don't think she has any idea of who you are. Alice is impressive too and without any medical training assisted you in curing my cancer."

"Alice has impressive powers of her own and I was able to use them when she merged with me during your treatment. I couldn't have done it without her help. Now, about your cancer. The new scans show no trace of it. There is some voids where the previous scans showed cancer, but these should fill in with time. Did you examine your breast to see or feel any difference?"

"Yes, it's as if the cancer was never there." Her eyes shined with unshed tears. "Thank you for saving me. I didn't want to worry my family until after I consulted with you, and my prayers were answered."

"Julia, I want to see you in a year for a follow-up examination. I don't expect to find anything, but it's better to play safe. This procedure Alice and I performed on you has never been done before and the hospital would like to tout how successful it was for you. Would you give us a release for PR purposes?"

"I'll give you one dated a week from now so that I can inform my family before the media gets it on the news."

"Wonderful! Where is your home located?"

"Omaha. I didn't have far to come here. I hope Alice and you continue in your efforts to help people."

After signing the release, Mrs. Clark and her two agents departed for home. I asked Alice, "What were you and Julia talking about before?"

"She was asking about my schooling and was surprised that I had almost three years of on-line undergraduate credits. She said her children were smart too, especially Marie, who wanted to be a doctor. She hoped that we would meet someday."

CHAPTER TWELVE

A week later Dr. Ellsworth made a news release to the local media outlets about the successful cancer treatment of Julia Clark, wife of former President Jason Clark. Within an hour of the release a TV news truck was parked outside the hospital and several print and TV reporters were requesting an interview.

Dr. Ellsworth arranged an interview in the hospital's conference room as soon as the media could set up. I mentally asked Alice, *Do you want to stand beside me for this interview?*

Why not. I think I'm ready for the spotlight and I'm like you in that I'm not a bit shy.

When everyone was ready, Dr. Ellsworth took the podium. "Tuesday of last week Mrs. Julia Clark was treated for ovarian and breast cancer. Dr. Angel Pearson-Blake, along with her daughter Alice, performed the procedure that left the patient cancer free. She was released the same day and returned to her home in Omaha, Nebraska. Are there any questions?"

A reporter from the *Kansas City Star* asked, "Dr. Pearson-Blake, is the young girl beside you Alice, and how old is she?"

"My daughter is eleven and she is very gifted. When I started the treatment she merged her mind with mine and helped me find the cancer cells that I removed. After we completed the task and were satisfied none remained, she returned to her body."

"This is almost unbelievable except for the fact that you have done so many other miracles in the past. Alice, how long have you had your powers?"

"I have had abilities almost since birth and have gained strength as I got older. I am still acquiring new gifts even now."

A local TV talking head asked, "Besides what you did with your mother, can you give a demonstration?"

Alice mentally asked me, *Shall I give this guy something he'll remember the rest of his life?*

Don't move him too far off the floor.

"Okay, how about this." The TV reporter lifted off the floor until he reached the end of his mike cord.

"Are you satisfied?"

"Yes, yes! Please let me down easy."

After everyone had quieted down I asked, "Any other questions?"

The *Star* reporter asked, "Do you plan on doing these types of treatments in the future?"

"Yes, I will consider them on an individual basis. Obviously, my time is limited because of my other commitments. We have an outstanding hospital here staffed by world class medical doctors and surgeons that provide treatment in addition to what my sister Elizabeth and I do. They will provide the majority of care and treatment for our patients."

"Can you tell us how many patients Elizabeth has cured last year and so far this year, and the same for your procedures?"

"I'll let Dr. Ellsworth take that question."

Dr. Ellsworth took my place at the podium. "I'll research that question and provide the answer to anyone who wants it if they leave me a name and email address. However, Elizabeth generally sees twenty or more every week, and Dr. Angel Pearson-Blake generally treats between six and eight patients daily, five days a week. The reason she can see so many patients is each treatment generally takes less than fifteen minutes; however, Mrs. Clark's procedure was almost forty minutes. You have to remember that she is the department head of Emergency Medicine, in addition to her unconventional medicine program."

There were several more questions relating to topics already answered before the news conference ended. I asked Alice, "Is there anything else you need to finish before heading home?"

"No. I imagine Grace is getting tired of waiting on me and Elizabeth has already left. I'll see you soon at home."

"Alright, have you decided what kind of physical exercise program you want to do?"

"Definitely not any kind of dance classes. Why not Judo, everyone else in the family has done it?"

"You don't need it for self-protection, so it's a purely self gratification activity. Don't use your gifts or your instructor will kick you out of the class. If you like I'll bring you with us when your dad and I go to our next class this evening."

"Okay, I'm looking forward to it."

Later, when we arrived at the *Greater Kansas City Martial Arts Center*, I introduced Alice to our instructor, Ming How. The two were about the same height, but Ming How was mostly muscle earned from long hours of practice. Ming How's face blanched in fear as she looked at Alice. "You much more powerful than mother and I thought she strong. You aura is dark purple, almost black. You no need me!"

Alice bowed to Ming How, causing her to back up slightly. "Ming How, I'm weak physically and knowing Judo is a family tradition. I promise not to use my gifts if you help me; however, I warn you I know some moves from watching my parents."

"Ha! You not ambush me with a move you not supposed to know, like your mother?"

Alice looked at me in surprise. "Mother, you wouldn't do that?"

"She surprised me and I used a move your grandmother taught me without thinking."

"She taught me some moves too, but I promise not to use them."

Ming How looked at Alice doubtfully. "You absolve me from bad karma when I give you pain?"

"Yes. Maybe I can demonstrate the moves I already know and then you can begin from that point."

Jeff and I watched as Ming How attacked and rebuffed Alice's moves, again and again, until she encountered a move from Alice she didn't know and found herself on the floor. Ming How quickly regained her feet and asked Alice to show her the move again in slow motion, but then asked, "Do you know this move daughter used?"

We both said no and had never seen it before either. Alice said, "I found it on the internet and I've never tried it before."

Ming How said, "Show me."

Ming How and Alice went through the same move several times before Ming How devised a countermove and was satisfied. "Now you demonstrate beginning move for daughter and I will see if she is good student she looks."

Twenty minutes later we were up to brown belt moves, but Alice was finished as far as her physical conditioning would allow. She sat against the wall watching as Jeff and I continued with our routines with Ming How. When we finished, Ming How drew us aside. "Daughter is prodigy. She learn faster than any I teach. You approve if Master Yow observe at her next session?"

We agreed and I took Alice with me to the showers. Her muscles had stiffened up while sitting and she limped beside me saying, "Ouch, ouch, oh that hurts."

"It will feel better when you get under the hot showers. Use my shoulder and we'll get there faster."

While we were under the showers I gave her sore muscles a quick massage and told her I'd do it better when we got home. Jeff looked at Alice with concern as we met later. "Alice, do you feel better after the shower?"

"Better, at least I can walk without too much pain. I didn't realize I was so out of shape. Ming How must be all muscle. Do you think I'll ever get even half as strong as she is?"

I said, "She's impressed by how quickly you learn and wants to show you off to Master Yow at your next lesson. He is the head of the Judo school and revered by his students and instructors."

"Really, the way she was throwing me around I thought she didn't like me."

"Honey, she considers you a brown belt after only one lesson. She's a little afraid of you and wants feedback from Master Yow."

"Oh. Should I dog it at the next lesson or be my normal self?"

"Be normal. When we enter the room where Master Yow is sitting, bow to show him respect. Follow my lead as I don't know what to expect."

The next week when we arrived at the Center, we were told to change into our uniforms and report to room 121 for a review by Master Yow. After changing and walking to our meeting, we could see two uniformed black belts outside the door we were to enter. I mentally reminded Alice, *remember to follow my lead.*

One of the black belts opened the door for us as we arrived. Master Yow was sitting in a chair on a raised platform at the far side of the large training room. At his side stood Ming How and the two black belts followed us inside, shutting the door behind us. We walked toward Master Yow until we were within fifteen feet, where we stopped and gave him a deep bow.

When we raised our heads he returned our bow. He then gave his full attention to Alice. "Alice, Ming How is impressed by your abilities, especially on how fast you are able to progress in only one training session. You resemble your mother except your aura, which show you as more powerful. That is disturbing because your mother is very powerful. At the time I considered her the most powerful person I had ever met. I saw your hospital's news conference and your ability to merge minds to destroy cancer cells. Two powerful people able to merge into a more powerful being. You have promised not to use your special abilities learning Judo, yet still you shine like a bright star. I would like you and Ming How spar for me so that I can judge for myself how you have advanced."

"Ming How, start where you left off at the last session."

Ming How and Alice bowed to each other and then Ming How showed Alice how to defend against the next attack. They moved apart and Ming How attacked and was rebuffed by Alice, then Alice was attacked by Ming How using a move taught last week. Alice and Ming How sparred, each trying to gain an advantage, before breaking apart.

"Master, she remember lesson from last week and has devise more counter moves than I teach her. She is good as me for the moves I teach. I about to reach my limit for her to advance."

Master Yow asked Alice, "What is your purpose in learning Judo? I sense it's not for self-defense."

"I want to expand my knowledge and make my body stronger. I don't need to advance any further, but since my parents are both black belts, it would be nice to reach that goal."

"Ming How can give you both a strong body and advancement to a black belt if that is all you desire. If later you want to advance higher, then a different instructor will be provided. Is that what you want?"

"Yes, Ming How is a good instructor even if she does give me more pain than I anticipated."

Ming How said, "No pain, no gain."

Master Yow said, "It's agreed then. Ming How will continue as your instructor until you decide otherwise."

Everyone gave Master Yow a bow and he left the room. Ming How said, "Begin?"

After Alice's and Ming How's bow to each other they returned to their lesson, and Jeff and I began our routine. Later, after the showers were over and they were walking to the car I asked Alice, "How do you feel, you don't seem as sore as you did last week?"

"You're right, I'm not. Maybe I didn't get thrown as much this time. I think Ming How backed off a little too. Maybe she felt sorry for me."

"I think Master Yow was very impressed with you. I don't think he wanted you to be angry with him."

"I got that impression as well, and that's without peeking into his mind."

We arrived at our Condo's underground parking garage and were walking toward the elevators, when we were surrounded by several men with threatening body language. Alice mentally asked, *how do you want to handle this? I can disable them all or we can use Judo on them and get some more exercise.*

You take care of them since there are at least eight of them. Let them talk first so we can get an idea what this is all about.

One of the threatening men cursed at us. "You are all abominations in the face of God and should be eliminated for preaching false claims in his name. When we are done with you no one will believe what you claim. Kill them!"

Before anyone could move there was a brilliant flash of light and Olivia with her magnificent spread wings stood before the attackers. "DO YOU RECOGNIZE AN ANGEL WHEN YOU SEE ONE STANDING BEFORE YOU?"

Her voice was so loud that it set car alarms off and the attackers stood with their mouths open. "ANSWER ME YOU SONS OF THE DEVIL. WHY DO YOU ATTACK GOD'S MESSENGERS?"

The leader of the attackers was shaking so hard that he had a hard time speaking, "Our leader told us they were not true God's messengers, but were really fakers who had no real power."

"DO I LOOK LIKE A FAKE ANGEL?"

"No! No! You are an angel from God."

"THEN YOUR LEADER IS THE ONE WHO GIVES FALSE TESTOMONY AND MUST BE THROWN OUT BEFORE HE DOES GREATER HARM. LEAVE HERE AND REMEMBER, GOD PREACHES LOVE AND NOT HATE."

The attackers left as quickly as they arrived and we were alone with Olivia, who turned to us and said, "I know Alice could have handled these misguided fools, but they spoke the key word 'kill' when referring to you. I believe this faction will no longer trouble you, but there are others remaining who are as misguided as these were. Stay vigilant as I will and continue to do God's work."

Olivia vanished in another flash of light and the car alarms stopped their clamoring, leaving us alone in a quiet garage. Alice said, "Wow! So that was Olivia. She's really impressive. What's next?"

I hugged her. "Let's order us something to eat and you can tell Elizabeth all about your experience."

CHAPTER THIRTEEN

Four years later brought additional changes in our family. Elizabeth, now twenty-four, was three years into undergraduate studies at Missouri University, Kansas City. She was not yet sure if she would try for a law or medical career since she still had healing powers, and Barbara has not given her any guidance. Alice, now fifteen, has not discovered any new powers, but she was much stronger in all her gifts. Alice and I had performed enough miracle treatments together during this period to earn us and the hospital a worldwide reputation as a place to seek treatment.

The hospital added another wing, which gave it the look of a big T. Dr. Ellsworth had to open a new section under the supervision of Emergency Medicine titled Urgent Care. These patients had overwhelmed the ER with their demands for service until it was either turn them away or place them elsewhere. Johns Hopkins Hospital now employed more medical staff than any other hospital in Kansas City.

Mother asked me and my family to come to dinner after work to discuss the future of Elizabeth and ourselves. We arrived from our short walk down the hallway from our own apartment. Elizabeth greeted us at the door and greeted Alice more like a younger sister than as an aunt. I gave her a hug too, but my relationship as her much older sister was not as close as what she had with Alice. "Mom and dad just got home from the office."

There was another knock on the door heralding the arrival of our meal. I helped by taking charge of the food, while Elizabeth paid the delivery man. I took the sacks into the kitchen while yelling that the food has arrived. I knew what everyone wanted to drink, so I prepared ice tea for everyone but Alice, who preferred water.

I was surprised when I opened the sacks of food and discovered that Mother had ordered us steak and all the trimmings. The girls set the table and I dug out the steak knives for them to add to the place settings. Mother and dad joined us and we all took our places at the table. Mother asked, "Angel, would you give the blessing tonight?"

I raised an eyebrow at her, but did as she asked. When I finished we all dug in with gusto as this was not our usual fare. I said, "Mother, this is really quite good. Have you used them before?"

"No, Marilyn told me about them. I'm glad I ordered this fine meal. It's a reward for all the hard work your father and I have put in on a case. They finished the meal and everyone pitched in for the cleanup, so they soon finished and were starting to walk toward the living area when Dad spoke, "I would like a picture of all the women standing before Barbara's painting in age order, Jenn you first on the left."

After we were all situated the way Dad wanted us, he took our picture. "Barbara Messing wanted this for a new painting."

Jeff looked at the screen showing our images. "It's almost unreal. You are all the same person at different stages of your lives."

We all looked at the screen and then at each other. I said, "Mother, everyone who sees us says the same thing, that we look alike. I'm thinking that there's a reason for this resemblance. Everyone, think about it - just look at us in this picture, there has to be a reason, an explanation."

All of us women turned to the painting of Barbara and Jenn said, "Sister, I think we need information about this and what's in store for Elizabeth and Alice?"

Barbara stepped out of her painting and stood before us. She looked at us for a moment, then said, "Mothers and daughters in a united front. That's as it should be, but I can see where your concern lies. Elizabeth is at the age where decisions regarding her future should be made. Elizabeth, you are going to retain your healing powers throughout your long life. You make what you like of your free time. Alice, you will continue to work with your mother, but because of your mind melds you both now have the same gifts. You need to go to medical school as well and take the shortcuts when they are offered. Angel needs you to help her as soon as possible. Now, as to why you all look alike, that's my fault. Jenn already looked like me, so I asked that you all looked like her, or me by extension. You are all beautiful women and anyone looking at you will know what lineage you are from."

Elizabeth asked, "How much free time am I going to have so that I can plan another vocation?"

"That's up to you and your conscience. If it's any help you have the same talent to paint as Barbara Messing."

Mother said, "Oh my!"

Barbara smiled at us and then disappeared back into her painting. Elizabeth and Alice both ran into their mother's arms with tears of joy in their eyes. I said, "Elizabeth, Dr. Bob Peterson is now working for Johns Hopkins and his girlfriend is Barbara Messing. The last I heard she has moved here to be close to him."

Dad said, "I'll give you her phone number if you want to call her. I can do it now when I send this picture I took to her?"

"Yes please. What am I going to say?"

Jenn said, "Tell her what you learned today and ask for her help in getting started."

Alice asked me, "Mother, we need to determine what I need to graduate from Missouri University and see if I can get into a medical school."

I looked at Mother and our eyes met. She then smiled at me. "Now you know how I felt when you were preparing to leave home when you were only fifteen. Welcome to motherhood."

The following day Alice and I were at the local campus of Missouri University speaking with an administrator about Alice's earned credits and what she needed to graduate. The final determination was that she lacked one three-credit course when this term ended, but she could test out if she thought she could pass the test.

I said, "Alice, did you check all your computer courses to see if you received credit at MU?"

Alice quickly examined the courses that were listed and mentally compared them with the computer courses she had completed. "I took a three-credit computer course four years ago that's not on this list. Maybe it was an oversight?"

The administrator asked, "Do you have documentation of the course?"

Alice opened her bag, leafed through several folders, then pulled out a folder that contained all the computer course transcripts she had completed. Alice handed over the transcript and waited for a determination.

"Well, this should be easy to check out since it's one of our courses." The administrator punched a few keys on her computer and she compared the transcript with the information on the screen.

"This checks out and that means you will graduate this spring. Congratulations on your accomplishment, I haven't seen many fifteen year-olds graduate from here."

Alice said, "I'll be sixteen by the time of graduation, but thanks for your help."

Later that day, we were in Dr. Ellsworth's office. "Janice, we have news from Barbara that relates to Alice and me. Barbara told us that because of our mind melding during our joint treatment of patients, that we each have acquired the talents of the other and I no longer need Alice when I do my treatments. Alice was told that she should attend medical school and take a fast track if it's offered. Barbara wants her back here to help me as soon as possible."

Dr. Ellsworth looked at us with her mouth open in surprise. "Oh my! When can she start medical school?"

"We just checked and Alice will graduate from MU this spring."

Janice's face brightened with a big smile. "I can hardly wait until I call President Smithson. Alice, you have no idea the impact your mother had on Johns Hopkins, both the university and hospital. She was only eighteen when she started there and you are even younger, what sixteen?"

Alice said, "Is this going to be good or bad news for him?"

"It's going to be a shock at first, then when he knows about your talents, he'll begin to fantasize about what your presence will mean for the school. Do you have a black belt in Judo like your mother?"

"Yes, why do you ask?"

I said, "Because you are going to be asked to instruct a self-defense class when you get there, the same as I did."

CHAPTER FOURTEEN

Six months later Mother and I were in the admissions office located in Mason Hall at Johns Hopkins University. The woman behind the desk asked my name and I replied, "Alice April Blake."

She handed me a packet. "You are housed in Wolman Hall for your freshman year and will have two roommates. Your faculty advisor will contact you by email to make an appointment to discuss your first semester class schedule. If you shipped anything here it should already be in your assigned room. Any questions?"

I looked at mother. "No questions. My name is Dr. Angel Pearson-Blake and I would like an appointment to talk to President Smithson while I'm here. Here's my email so that I can be reached."

"Oh, Dr. Pearson-Blake. He left a message for you and your daughter to meet with him at six tonight in his office. Do you know where it's located?"

"Remind me in case it's moved since I was there last."

"That's the same location I remembered, so if there's nothing else we'll leave."

"Wait a minute. Are you the famous Angel that the rumors say is coming back?"

"I see that the rumor mill is as misleading as it was when I was here. It may seem like I'm coming back, but it's a new better version of me in the form of my daughter."

The admissions officer paled as she looked at us. "You even look alike."

After we left the building I asked, "Mom, how far is it to the residence hall?"

"Not far, maybe a fifteen minute walk. Let's stop at the rec room for something to drink. It's on the way."

I followed Mother into the building housing the rec room and was pleased at how large it was and surprised at the number of people sitting and talking with each other. I asked, "Who are all these people, surely they aren't freshmen."

"No, these are mostly upperclassmen students who are getting reacquainted with friends. Drinks are over here. Coffee, tea, or soft drink?"

We each picked out our choice and found a table to ourselves. "Mom, is this where you spent your free time?"

"I spent most of my out of class time in my room studying, but there were times I came here to unwind and talk to friends. One of the reasons I opened a checking account for you here was that you'll probably be asked to consult at the hospital on special cases. They paid me $10,000 for each consult, but initially it was only $5,000. President Smithson felt guilty that a member of his staff tried to have me killed. Because of that, my tuition and dorm room were free. Don't expect that for yourself."

When we arrived at my dorm room, Mother said, "My old room was just down the hall. I hope your experience here will be as satisfying as it was for me."

When we entered the room we found we were alone, but the floor was covered with boxes, some of it mine. Mother helped me find my boxes and we set them apart from the others. "Alice, which bedroom do you want?"

"The center one, just like you picked."

We had just finished unpacking and straightening up the room when there was a knock and Mother yelled, "Enter!"

My first roommate entered. "Are you my two roommates?"

I laughed. "I am. My name is Alice and this is my mother, Dr. Angel Pearson-Blake and we're from Kansas City."

"Hi, my name is Candy Thompson and I'm from Chicago. You really look young, how old are you?"

"Sixteen, but I feel older." I said with a grin.

"Wow! Is that a record for entering med school? Am I meeting another Doogie Howser?"

Mother said, "I started here when I was eighteen, so she may be a record holder."

Candy looked at Mother, then did a double-take. "You are the famous mother/daughter healers from Kansas City. Wow, Alice what are you doing here?"

"Well, first of all we're not healers in the way you mean. My Aunt Elizabeth is the healer. We do surgery without cutting into the body."

Candy's eyes got even bigger. "So it's true, you are famous. But why medical school? Oh, it's obvious. As a pair your mother was the doctor, but you can't act alone without the formal training."

Candy was a small woman, just over five feet, and was a brunette with a slim athletic body. She looked at me, then my mother before asking, "If I remember correctly, one or both of you is a black belt in something. Am I right?"

I said, "We both have black belts in Judo. How about you, do you have self-defense training?"

"No. As small as I am I should get some kind of training. I wonder if they have classes here?"

"Mother taught Judo when she was a student here. Maybe someone will have a class, maybe even me."

There was another knock and my other roommate arrived. We introduced each other and she told us her name was Viola Simpson from Santa Fe. She was slightly shorter than me, was of apparent mixed blood with her mother being either Hispanic or American Indian, because of her dusky skin color. She was quite beautiful and had a curvaceous body and dark curly hair.

She looked at me curiously for a moment, then Candy retold our history. "So you are here to get your formal training to do what you already know how to do."

"Viola, it might seem that way, but I still have a lot to learn. Maybe we can help each other out in our studies. Let's start by getting the contents of these boxes into your rooms."

After they finished putting their rooms in order I asked them to come into the common room. After everyone was seated I showed them my copy of Barbara's painting. "Do you mind if I hang this in the common room? Before you give me an answer I should give you the history of this painting. The original is a self-portrait of my great aunt who died shortly after giving it to my grandfather, who she was engaged to. My grandfather eventually married Barbara's younger sister, my mother's mother. Jenn and my grandfather hadn't met since Barbara's funeral until she met him again in Kansas City on her first day on the job as an Assistant Attorney General. My grandfather was her supervisor and they were married within two weeks. Barbara is now a messenger angel from God and has spoken to everyone in our family and those close to us. I wanted her picture with me to advise me on important matters."

Candy said, "You're pulling my leg! Does she appear and talk to you or do you just hear her in your head?"

"Both. When I was younger she talked to me in my dreams."

Viola said, "Don't be so quick to judge. I believe in angels and you don't have to be religious to see them."

Barbara was with us before Viola stopped speaking, causing my roommates to gasp in surprise. "Alice, these young women appear to be of strong character, but Candy seems to have forgotten her Sunday school lessons. Now that question of my being real is settled, do you take exception to my picture being hung in this room?"

Candy asked, "Can I touch you to make sure I'm not seeing things?"

Barbara walked over and touched Candy's hand. "Are you satisfied?"

Viola grabbed Candy's hand. "Don't piss off an angel or you'll live to regret it."

I said, "You're thinking of Olivia, my guardian angel. She's the one you don't want to get mad at you, but she doesn't appear unless I'm in mortal danger."

Barbara said, "Alice, be quiet. Don't scare your friends for no reason. Actually, if you stay close to Alice you will always be safe because of her protection or Olivia's. I would prefer that you not bring boys into your rooms for sex. Do that elsewhere because she's still a minor. If a boy should be too aggressive with her she might overreact and do him harm. Do you understand?"

My roommates nodded and together said, "No boys in the

bedrooms."

Barbara disappeared and my roommates breathed a sigh of relief. They looked at Mother and Candy asked. "When you were here you had a picture too?"

"Yes."

"Barbara makes a good chaperon, doesn't she?"

"She used my roommates to make sure I stayed on the straight path God had planned for me. When I asked her for advice she never told a lie, and when I asked a straight question she usually gave me the answer I wanted unless it wasn't in my best interest to know. She would then explain why she couldn't tell me at that time."

Mother then said, "Alice and I have a meeting with President Smithson at six, do you want to have an early dinner with us at Nolan's, my treat."

On the walk to the restaurant Mother explained that it was on the ground floor of Charles Commons dormitory, one of the most sought-after dormitories by upper classmates. She said the food was the best on campus, at least when she was here about twenty years ago.

When we were seated, Mother said, "They've redone the restaurant. It's at least twice the size it was before and I saw several more dormitories. The school must have more students now."

I was used to eating out since my parents worked long hours and didn't have time to cook. I took Mother's advice and ordered the Chef's salad, which was really more than I could eat. My roommates both ordered a steak, which they said was excellent. We talked about each other's background. Viola's father was an attorney and real estate investor who had accumulated sufficient wealth to afford sending his daughter to this university. Her mother had died in an accident over ten years ago and raised her daughter in the Catholic faith.

Candy, which was a nickname for Candice, was raised in a family of doctors. Both of her parents and grandparents were doctors. That's how she knew of Mother's and my medical fame. Her parents read everything in print about our treatments and were considering making a trip to Kansas City to learn how we treated our patients.

Mother said, "Tell them it's not anything that can be taught.

We got our abilities from God and we use our minds to explore our patients' bodies looking for cancer cells to eradicate or make needed adjustments to their internal organs. As soon as Alice completes her medical training she will join me and we will both continue separately what we had previously done together. With her we will more than double our case load."

After leaving my roommates at the restaurant we walked around the campus where she pointed out various points of interest and where the hospital was located. Eventually, we arrived outside the building where President Smithson's office was located and found a bench to sit, as we had about fifteen minutes until our appointment.

Mother had told me about sitting on a bench enjoying the seasonal scents and watching the students walk by. I must really be my mother's daughter because I too was enjoying the quiet until an older man stopped before us. "Angel, I see you continue your old habits. This can only by your daughter Alice. She looks so much like you it's unsettling. Excuse me Alice, I'm President Raymond Smithson and I want to welcome you to our university. I hope your stay here will be satisfying and uneventful, but somehow I don't think uneventful is going to happen. Come, let's continue this conversation in my office."

When mother and I stood, she embraced Smithson and kissed his cheek. "It's been too long. Are you feeling well?"

He smiled at her. "You tell me?"

"You appear in good shape considering your age. Your heart, lungs, and other major organs are functioning well. How much exercise have you been getting?"

Smithson winked at me. "Your mother has turned into a mother hen."

"She does that for everyone she cares about. She keeps after Dr. Ellsworth too."

While looking at me Smithson took a step and stumbled over a raised crack in the sidewalk. As he started to fall we both automatically reached out with our minds and steadied him. He looked at us. "Which one of you saved me from a fall?"

I said, "We both did. In some things we are of the same mind."

"Just as I thought, this is going to be another interesting time for the university."

When we got to Dr. Smithson's office he had us take a seat while we waited for another party to arrive. Mother and Smithson were catching up when there was a knock on the door and a woman entered. Dr. Smithson introduced her as my advisor, Dr. Samantha Hogan. She appeared to be in her late thirties or early forties, short ash blond hair, about my height and had an athletic body. She took a seat and seemed a little confused as to why she was here.

Smithson said, "Dr. Hogan, this older person is the famous Dr. Angel Pearson-Blake, who finished her residency here about twenty years ago. She came to us when she was only eighteen and now we have her daughter, who is sixteen. Angel, when she was younger was a healer. When she was fifteen she lost that ability, but was given the ability to diagnose health problems by touch. You can imagine the advantage this would give us when time was critical. We used her in the hospital as a paid consultant while she was here. She graduated in three and half years as her class valedictorian. "

"Before she completed her residency here she persuaded me and the Board to approve establishing a satellite Johns Hopkins Hospital in Kansas City. Surely, you have heard what she has done since its opening. Her daughter is much more powerful than Angel was when she started here. They want Alice placed on a fast track to graduate in three years or less to be followed by a short residency at JH Hospital. Before coming here she was performing treatments with her mother that involved mind melding where they combined their abilities to perform miracle treatments. Dr. Ellsworth, your predecessor, informed me that this mind melding has resulted in them transferring their abilities to each other. The effect being that Alice or Angel can now do what it used to require both of them to do. However, Alice needs medical training to perform these tasks legally."

I said, "I need more medical knowledge as well. I have an eidetic memory and remember everything about the treatments I performed with Mother, but if I encounter anything new I would need help."

Dr. Hogan looked at me with speculation. "What powers do you have?"

I mentally asked mother, *should I tell her everything we can do?"*

At her mental okay, I said, "I can mentally talk to other people and read their surface thoughts, I have the ability to move items with my mind, I can scan for specific cells and mentally highlight them for eradication, and everything else Mother could do."

Smithson said, "I met them outside and when we started walking here. I stumbled and they both kept me from falling with their minds."

 Dr. Hogan said, "How high is your IQ and you say you have an eidetic memory?"

"Over 200, tests are not accurate when it's that high. All the women in our family line have eidetic memories and high IQ's."

"Very well. Your class load will be heavy and it will mean taking summer school, but you need to take breaks when possible to keep your mind fresh. No distractions, like boys if this is going to work."

Mother shook her head, causing me to ask, "What?"

"I had almost eight years of unconsummated love for your father because Barbara kept telling us that it wasn't time yet for marriage because we needed to concentrate on my studies. I hope you don't get caught in the same situation that I did."

"But you did know that eventually you would marry him. I don't even have a prospect, but I'd rather be lonely than pining for a guy that I can't have."

Dr. Hogan said, "Let me have your email address and I'll let you know where and when we should meet for your class schedule. You said you could read surface thoughts of people, tell me what I'm thinking."

"You think I'm full of myself, now you're thinking nobody is smart enough to carry this heavy a load of classes, now you're trying to block your thoughts."

"Can I block my thoughts from you?"

"Sure, just don't think of anything, or hum a song to yourself."

"What's your range?"

"Untested. I hope to be able to talk to Mother in Kansas City. We communicated between ourselves from the hospital to home, that's about fifteen miles."

President Smithson said, "Alice, would you be willing to

consult with doctors from our hospital?"

"Yes, but my free time is going to be limited because of my heavy schedule. Is there going to be a fee arrangement like with mom?"

"Yes, would the same fee be agreeable?"

"Yes. I also would like the same arrangement you had with Mom about the use of my blood. Depending on my schedule I would be agreeable to teaching a self-defense class as I, like my mother, hold a black belt in Judo. It might be a way for me to release tension from classes."

Smithson said, "I'll re-issue that original memo I sent out for your mother. Dr. Hogan, be sure that the appropriate person is notified for that class. Is there anything else we need to discuss now? If not, I look forward to see how you handle yourself here."

CHAPTER FIFTEEN

After mother and I left President Smithson's office we sat at the same bench we had before meeting him. Mother held my hand. "This is the hardest thing I've ever done, leaving my young daughter alone to fend for herself. I was in your shoes when I entered MU at fifteen, but I immediately found Lilly who took care of me. You're only a year older and it's tearing me apart."

I hugged Mother. "Mom, remember I'm only a thought away and if that doesn't work we each have a cell phone. I can take care of myself and when I get lonely I'll talk to you. You can always ask Barbara how I'm getting along."

Mother wiped her eyes and then used a tissue to wipe mine. We touched our foreheads together, each saying a silent prayer that we both heard. We each kissed the other on the cheek before Mother hailed a cab to catch a late flight back to Kansas City, while I slowly walked back to my dorm. It was dusk, almost dark as I walked along the winding sidewalk where I saw few students at this hour on the first day of enrollment. I met a man at a intersection of the sidewalk I was following and he started following me.

I probed his mind and found he was concerned for me because of my young age, so I stopped and confronted him. "I'm a freshman too, are you lost or just want company?"

"I'm not lost, but I thought maybe you were. You look too

young to be a student here."

"I'm sixteen, but I'm pretty smart and able to take care of myself. I have a black belt in Judo plus other abilities. My name is Alice Blake, what's yours?"

"Bob Jackson, from Branson, Missouri. Where are you from?"

"Kansas City, so we're from the same State."

He laughed. "Just barely. Both of us live on the State line of other States. Maybe if we have the same class we can study together."

"It's possible, but I will be carrying a heavy load, so most of my time is spoken for. I'll be teaching a self-defense class in Judo, if you're interested."

"So you really do know Judo? I thought you were just trying to ward me off."

"Are you staying at McCoy Hall too?"

"Yeah. My father stayed there when he attended classes here."

"We have that in common. My mother was also here. Maybe you've heard of her, Dr. Angel Pearson-Blake."

Bob stopped abruptly and looked at me intently. "The mother and daughter team at Johns Hopkins in Kansas City. Is that you and your mother?"

"Guilty as charged. Is that good or bad news for you?"

"When you said you had other abilities you weren't kidding. I've read up on you and your mother and I saw the news program where you used your mind to raise that newsman off the floor. That was mind blowing. I didn't know that was even possible. Why do you teach Judo, you don't need it for defense?"

"Both my parents were black belts and I wanted to see if I could do it. I needed exercise and this served both objects. It's also a way for me to release tension."

"You weigh what, 105 pounds. You can throw a guy like me weighing 170 pounds?"

"No problem. If that doesn't work I can throw you twenty feet with my other powers."

"Wow, I'll make sure I'm near you if muggers show up."

We said our goodbyes in the elevator before he got off first. I knocked on my door and received a "come in" before opening the door and greeting my roommates. "I met a nice guy while walking back to the dorm and he's from my home state."

Viola said, "Alice, you're supposed to stay away from boys. Did he try to pick you up?"

"No, he was concerned that I was so young and walking alone. He was protective until he realized who I was."

"What's his name so I can check him out?"

"Hey guys, chill out. Remember I can read his surface thoughts. He's for real and his name is Bob Jackson and is really nice. His father is a doctor and went to school here too."

Candy said, "You said he knows who you are? Was it through his father like me?"

"No, remember he lives in Missouri too, and was fascinated by the news coverage of Mother and my medical procedures that didn't involve cutting into the body. He was in awe that I was here attending medical school."

My roomies looked at me for a moment before Viola said, "You're going to get a lot of that, and not just because of your age."

* * *

I consulted with Dr. Hogan on my class schedule and I selected seven courses totaling sixteen hours for my first semester. Dr. Hogan said, "You're carrying more credits than any other student, but you can scale back next semester if it's too much for you. Three of the courses didn't require much study time, but the others more than made up for them. With your eidetic memory it might be helpful to read your study books before attending class; however, that's only three days away."

I started reading the text book of what I considered to be my toughest course based on my mental conversations with Mother. Apparently, this ability was not affected by the distance between Kansas City and Baltimore. By start of classes on Monday I had read all the books for my classes.

My first class was a combined Anatomy/Physiology course taught by Dr. Elizabeth Parsons. Mother warned me that she wanted not only the correct answer, but the reasons behind the answer. When I entered the large classroom I was not surprised by the small number of students present because Mother had informed me this combined class was only for students with high IQ's. My mother had helped Dr. Parsons start the class to keep it from being boring.

I knew to take a seat up front next to a male student that I was surprised to see was Bob Jackson. I only had enough time to say hi before our instructor arrived. Dr. Parsons looked out at her twelve students and grimaced. "Everyone move down next to and behind Ms. Blake and Mr. Jackson. I want three rows of four students."

After everyone had settled in their new seats, Dr. Parsons said, "We have a celebrity in our class. Ms. Alice Blake please stand and face your fellow students. For those of you who haven't been watching the news, Ms. Blake is one-half of a mother/daughter team who practices surgery without cutting at our satellite hospital in Kansas City. I want a show of hands of those who have heard of them."

All eleven held up their hands. Dr. Parsons said, "Ms. Blake is quite young. My records show she is sixteen, which is the youngest student to ever start at Johns Hopkins. Tell me Ms. Blake, why break up your successful team?"

"An angel told us that because of our mind melding in performing our treatments that we both had acquired the abilities of the other. I was instructed to obtain medical training so that I could perform the treatments separately from my mother, which would more than double our patient capacity."

Dr. Parsons said, "For everyone's information, Alice's mother, when she attended class here was known as Angel Pearson. She graduated in three and half years as her class' Valedictorian. She had such a big footprint that everyone in the University and Hospital knew of her and held her in awe, including me. This class is partially through her efforts because she thought the normal class was boring. You notice the class is small, that's because you have to have a genius IQ to enter. Alice Blake not only has all her mother's talents but those extra talents she was born with, which includes the ability to read minds and move objects mentally. Angel had a black belt in Judo which she used several times to protect herself and others. Alice has that plus her other talents. It would be wise of you to become her best friend and stay close to her so that she can defend you."

The shocked faces looking at me caused me to try to lighten

the mood, so I smiled at them and bowed. This caused one of the women to giggle and then they all started to laugh. I sat down relieved that they wouldn't fear me.

When the class was over I had an hour before my next class started and at their urging I followed most of the class to the rec room. We found a big table that seated everyone and while most of them drank coffee or tea, I had a soda. One of the women asked me, "Weren't you scared coming here when you are so young?"

"If you mean being on my own without parental support, remember I can read thoughts and even though my parents are in Kansas City, I can mentally talk to Mother when I like and if I need to talk to Dad, I'll use my cell. If you mean do I get lonely? I have a feeling we won't have time to be lonely with all the studying we'll have to do."

Bob said, "Yeah, I'm taking ten hours and that's going to keep me busy. How about the rest of you?"

Most in the class were taking ten hours, with the highest at eleven. Bob asked me, "What about you. How many are you taking?"

"Sixteen hours. But, I'm trying to graduate in three years."

"That's a killer load. Are you sure you can handle it?"

"We'll see. My advisor said I could lighten the load next semester if it's too hard. On a lighter note, if anyone is interested I'm teaching a self-defense class beginning this Wednesday evening at six in the gym. Call Dr. Kilpatrick and put your name on the list soon as I have room for only twenty students."

* * *

After a month of classes I found that I could handle the work load and still had time to find a quiet place and meditate, letting my mind expand and skim a little of the essence of others' auras. After each meditation I felt mentally stronger.

* * *

I turned to Jeff and said, "I just mentally talked to Alice and she seems grounded and happy with her class load. Her roommates have been recruited by Barbara to watch after her and have become close friends."

I hesitated a moment before continuing. "She mentions a freshman boy from Branson, Bob Jackson, whose father is a doctor. However, I think they're only friends. Do you think we should check up on him and his background?"

"Angel, remember she can read his surface thoughts. If they are friends, then she is satisfied with his character. Have they called her in on a consultation yet?"

"No. She says that she has several hours each day that she could fit that into if asked. She even likes teaching a self-defense class, but had to limit attendance to twenty students."

"Jeff, she's stronger mentally than me at her age. She's more self-reliant and sure of herself than I was too."

"She is her mother's daughter in all things, especially since you share her gifts. You and she are the same strong person I remember when I first met you. She is a younger you. When she is older she will have the same feelings you had when she meets her future mate. You can advise her on what she needs to do."

CHAPTER SIXTEEN

My phone chimed that I had an email. I was told to call Dr. Westerfield to make an appointment for a consultation. I was in the library doing some research for a class, so I emailed Westerfield back with the time of my next free period, which was answered immediately with a request to meet at the hospital, room 218, at my convenience.

Later, I knocked on the door of room 218. At the voice command to enter I found a woman sitting at a desk wearing a lab coat with Westerfield stenciled on it. I introduced myself and asked what the consult was about.

Dr. Westerfield was a slender woman about my mother's age, with dark hair pulled into a pony tail. She said, "How old are you?"

"Sixteen, but that has no bearing on what I can do."

"No, that's not the reason for my question. I have a daughter your age and there is no comparison between you and her except age." Westerfield's eyes filled with tears as she looked at me.

"I'm sorry. Is it drugs or normal acting out teenager?"

"The latter, but that's not why I need you. I have a patient that I have a problem diagnosing because of the conflicting symptoms."

She started to give me what her symptoms were when I held up my hand. "At this point in my training it would mean nothing to me. I need to touch the patient."

"Can you tell me what you sense when you touch someone?"

"If something is wrong I feel an uneasiness and a direction to search. Sometimes I just know what the problem is and head directly to the source. Others I start at the head and work down to the feet, sometimes finding multiple problems. I have a feeling that's the case here. Shall we?"

The patient was a twenty-five-year-old woman whose body seemed to be wasting away. I stopped at the entrance and looked around the ICU unit. "Are you sure she's not contagious?"

"No, I don't think so. She's been here a week and no one else has gotten sick."

"I want to suit up until after I touch her. If she's contagious, I wouldn't be able to return to my classes."

We both suited up and I touched her arm through the gloves I wore. I felt an ugly wrongness that I had never experienced before as I started my search. I took my time as I slowly scanned her body. I indicated that I was finished and we left the patient.

When we were back at Westerfield's office I told her I had never experienced this person's illness before. "I started at her brain and worked down and all her major organs are deteriorating. She's hours away from dying. What is her family situation? Does she have children?"

"She's married and has two young children."

"Wait a moment; I need to mentally consult with my mother."

Mom! I need your advice. I'm consulting on a patient who will die in a matter of hours and there is no treatment that would save her in the time allowed. She is a young mother with small children.

The decision is yours to make. Barbara told me that my blood had properties to protect me from illness and should only be used to help others in rare instances. I've done it twice and found that a small amount of our blood will work, like getting a flu shot. Honey I feel for you, but doctors sometimes have to make these life and death decisions.

"My mother told me I had to make the decision on whether or not I save this woman by giving her some of my blood."

After several minutes of contemplation, with tears running down my face I said, "I have to give her my blood for my own peace of mind. Draw a syringe of blood from me and give it to her. Assuming she recovers we need to track her future health. She will be the third person who has received blood from our line. Fax the patient's medical information to Dr. Angel Pearson-Blake, who is tracking their progress. Would you email me after you determine which way the patient's health is progressing? It may take several hours."

We went to the lab and drew my blood, and I watched as Dr. Westerfield injected it into the patient's arm. I started to leave, then had a thought. "What's your daughter's name?"

"Nancy."

I pulled my phone out and checked my schedule. "Bring her to my Judo session at the gym next Wednesday at five p.m. I have a plan that might work with her."

The next morning I received an email from Dr. Westerfield saying that the patient who received my blood had shown marked improvement, and was expected to recover.

Wednesday afternoon I was waiting in my gi, ready for my students who were to arrive later. Dr. Westerfield arrived a few minutes early with her daughter in tow. Nancy was close to my height, but a little slimmer and like me her body was just now starting to develop. I walked up to her and stuck out my hand. "Hi Nancy, I'm Alice. What grade are you in school?"

"Sophomore at Madison High. What's that outfit you're wearing?"

"It's a uniform or gi for people who practice martial arts. I'm a black belt in Judo and teach a class in self-defense."

"You teach. But, you're about my age."

"My mother and I both got our black belts when we were fifteen. My maternal grandparents both have black belts too. It just takes practice and builds the muscles in your body."

Nancy turned to her mother. "Is she for real? Is she who she says she is?"

"Yes dear. She's that and so much more."

"Can you show me what you do? I might be interested in taking a class."

"I have some extra uniforms stored in the locker room. I can suit you up and show you how to toss me around."

Nancy agreed and I took Dr. Westerfield aside and whispered that I wanted to talk to her daughter alone. I led Nancy back to the locker room and found a uniform that fit her. After she was dressed in the uniform, I showed her how the white belt was tied. "I can teach you how to defend yourself against those bullies at school. Pick out the worst and publicly defeat her, then the rest will leave you alone. It's going to take several lessons before you'll be ready, but you can do it!"

"How did you know about those bullies? Did mom find out and tell you?"

I hugged her shoulders. "I can read your surface thoughts. It's one of my talents. Ask your mother about me and my family later. We were given talents by God to help others and I've decided to help you if you will let me."

She looked at me and smiled. "Let's do it."

We rejoined Nancy's mother and I started showing her several defensive moves for when she would be rushed or someone would try to strike her. When I was sure she had the basics I had her rush me and I threw her over my head. I helped her up and asked if she was okay, and at her nod I told her it was her turn to throw me. I made it scary, with me yelling and holding my arms out toward her as I ran at her. She grabbed my gi and fell backwards using her feet to assist me fly over her. I did a tuck and roll maneuver to land on my feet and helped her to her feet.

"Now, If someone comes at you with the intention of pulling your hair, like this." I demonstrated by reaching for her head with both hands. "Use the heel of your hand to strike the person under their chin, Use sufficient force to knock them back, but don't try to kill them. Here, strike my hand and I'll tell you when it's right."

Her first try was not hard enough, the second was just right. "Alright, you're doing good." I then demonstrated a side throw when rushed in tight quarters and three other defenses against fighting attacks. I noticed that Nancy was starting to slow down as her strength was flagging and called an end to this session.

I bowed to her, which she reciprocated, then we both turned to Dr. Westerfield. "Mom! I learned to defend myself. Alice tells me I need more lessons and I really like doing this."

Westerfield asked, "Can you fit her into your class or should I enroll her elsewhere?"

"My class is full, but I'll take her. Nancy and I have an understanding on what she needs. Nancy, you'll need to take a hot shower to relieve your aching muscles. Why don't you and your mother go do that and she'll get you what you need. Be back here next Wednesday at six p.m. and bring a clean uniform. When you finish your shower you may watch my regular class if you like."

* * *

Driving home from the Judo lesson I asked, "Nancy, what did you and Alice talk about when you were changing into your uniform?"

"Mom did you know she can read your surface thoughts? She knew I was being harassed by bullies and told me I was her good deed project. She's going to get me ready to turn the tables on those mean girls who have been giving me trouble. Alice said to ask you about her and her family's history."

"I was a few years ahead of her mother when we attended Johns Hopkins University and residency at the hospital. Her mother's name was Angel and she was amazing. She consulted with the hospital staff on difficult patients because of her ability to diagnose health problems by touch. One of the staff got into trouble trying to coerce her into using her blood to cure a patient and when that failed he tried to have her killed. She like Alice, taught a Judo class and one of those attempts on her life was while she was teaching her class. There were four attackers and she rallied three of her brown belt students to help defeat them without injury to her class. Angel's sister is a healer by touch. Alice has Angel's abilities plus many others."

"Wow! Mom that seems almost unreal. The daughter following in the footsteps of her mother. Do you think I'd be a good doctor?"

* * *

A year later I was competing in the annual College Olympics. In my freshman year my entry scores were not high enough to compete, but this year I made my Daniel Nathans college team. Mom was a member of the Vivien Thomas college team, which won the two years she competed. I was the only sophomore competing on the teams, with the large majority being seniors. Team members are selected by taking an entry test and the four high scores from each college become members, with the high scorer the captain. Our team came in second to the Helen Taussig team by ten points. Since I was graduating in two more years, next year would be my last chance to be on a winning team.

I received an email from my advisor, Dr. Hogan, telling me that my high GPA has earned me a position on the team of ten students who will tour the hospital's various departments with the idea toward possible intern and residency when they graduate. The ten students would then answer questions from the student body. I was to report Saturday morning to Dr. Julia Song of Emergency Medicine.

Mom told me of her first exposure to the ER under Dr. Song and I knew how strict she was about her rules, much like Mom was in her ER. The ten of us crowded into a small conference room and were told what we were going to do by Dr. Reese Hull, Dr. Song's lead resident.

"Before we begin I want to call each person's name so that I may learn what you look like."

He had just started the roll call when Dr. Song entered the room. When he called my name and I held my hand up, I could feel her eyes on me. When Dr. Hull finished calling names, he introduced Dr. Song.

Dr. Song hesitated a moment before looking straight at me. "Ms. Blake are you any relation to Dr. Angel Pearson-Blake?"

"Yes ma'am. She is my mother."

"Then you should be aware of my ER rules for interns. Please tell your fellow students what they are."

I stood and took a breath. "If you faint at the sight or smell of blood, then you don't belong here. Everyone will wear a gown and gloves and stay out of the way of staff. When a staff member asks you to move, you move against the wall out of the way. You don't talk except to answer questions from the staff. Take notes after you leave the ER."

Dr. Song turned to Dr. Hull. "Did she miss anything?"

"She added the take notes part."

Dr. Song said, "Student's, Ms. Blake was until she started school here, half of a mother/daughter medical team at Johns Hopkins Hospital in Kansas City. Their miracle cures involving what used to be considered inoperable cancer is now known worldwide. I considered Dr. Angel Pearson my protégé when she was a resident here. Their mind melding process that they used in their procedure had a side effect of transferring their individual gifts to each other. Ms. Blake needs to earn her doctorate to be able to rejoin her mother and continue their practice so that separately they could heal more patients. I'm telling you this so that you may observe some things you probably won't see again in your lifetime. Dr. Hull, take your students on their tour of my ER."

When the tour was finished, Dr. Hull escorted me to Dr. Song's office, where he left us. Song pointed to a chair, where I sat and waited for her to get to the point of our meeting. "Angel called me last week and informed me of what was coming my way, a doctor much more powerful than she was at the time. She told me she wanted her daughter back properly trained in ER procedures because she was needed there to work in the ER and do miracle treatments on her own. Did you know of her plans for you in the ER?"

"No, but I guessed where this was heading. Mother's time in the ER is eroded by the demands of her other duties. She loved her time supervising the ER and she wouldn't leave it in the hands of someone she didn't trust. I'm thinking that she's trusting you to get me ready for that position as fast as you can. I'm going to be graduating a year early, so I'll start my internship a year after next. Have you been following my consultations here?"

"You do unbelievable work. It didn't take me long to suspect who you must be, but I kept quiet because I didn't want the other departments seeking you out. But really, your talents only fit here."

CHAPTER SEVENTEEN

Two years later I was ready to start my internship with Emergency Medicine after securing a special approval to work in only one department. President Smithson used my special abilities as justification. It didn't hurt that I had completed medical school in three years and graduated with special honors including Valedictorian of my class.

My parents came for my graduation and brought my aunt, Elizabeth, who was more like a sister because of our ages. Before the graduation ceremony we showed Elizabeth around the campus and the hospital where I would soon be working. We were taking a break at the rec room when Elizabeth took my arm and asked me to go to the restroom with her.

Once inside she pulled me over into a corner. "I've got a boyfriend! He's really handsome."

Surprised, I asked, "Where did you meet him?"

"He's a new doctor at the hospital, Dr. Wesley Graham. He goes by Wes and so far we've only hung out at the hospital."

"Has he tried to kiss you or indicated that he's hot for you?"

Elizabeth blushed. "No silly, we're hardly ever alone, but I can tell he likes me."

"Well, play it cool and if he's really interested he'll make the first move. Are you on the pill?"

"Noo! I'm not ready for that. I may only be imagining his

interest in me. Besides, I should be giving you love advice since I'm four years older. Have you got a love interest?"

"Are you kidding me? Not with the work load I'm carrying. I've got several male friends, but no romance."

"Alice, I'm beginning to think we're going to end up as old maids without ever having a husband."

"Our mothers found love and as soon as my residency is over I'm going hunting."

"Oh Alice, you're so full of it."

"Wait and see. As soon as I get back to Kansas City we'll go hunting together."

When we got back to the table I mentally told mom, *Elizabeth may have a boyfriend, a Dr. Wesley Graham. It may be nothing, but check him out mentally.*

Mom asked me, "Whatever happened to that student you liked, his name was Bob Jackson wasn't it?"

"Yeah, he's from Branson. Neither one of us had time for romance, but we remained friends. He'll graduate next year and he wants to intern at Cox Hospital in Springfield, Missouri, which is near Branson."

"Do you think he'll want to do his residency at our hospital?"

"Mom, can you do that? He might go for that since it's in the same State."

"Ask him and if he's agreeable, you might eventually be working together."

I returned home to Kansas City after graduation for a short break before I started my internship. I was in Elizabeth's bedroom where she was showing me some of her recent paintings. Many were still life, but the one I liked the best was a self-portrait where she was looking at herself in a mirror. Except for the hair style it could have been me. Her lonely eyes drew me to the painting.

Elizabeth stood beside me as we looked at the self-portrait. I put my arm around her shoulder and gave her a hug, causing her eyes to shine with unshed tears. I said, "Enough of this, let's go talk to Barbara."

Holding her hand I led her into the living room where we stood before Barbara's painting. I said, "Elizabeth is lonely and needs a husband. Is there any hope on the horizon for either of us?"

Barbara suddenly was standing in front of us and held out her arms, and we both moved into her embrace. She held us both to her breasts until our emotions settled. She moved back a step and used her hands to raise our chins so that we were looking into her eyes. "Elizabeth, you've grown up so fast and I can see how lonely you are, but you will soon meet the man who will be your mate. You will know him by a jolt to your body, so don't ignore the clue. Immediately show an interest in him and he will respond in kind. Alice, be sure and follow up on your mother's offer to Mr. Jackson. At this point he's your best opportunity."

She then kissed our cheeks and returned to the painting. Elizabeth and I looked at each other and then screamed in happiness as we hugged. Elizabeth suddenly sobered. "Who's this Jackson?"

"Bob Jackson, he's a fellow student who's from Branson, Missouri. Both of us have been busy with classes, but we see each other in classes together and sometimes when we are taking a break in the rec room."

"Call him and invite him to come here soon, tomorrow if you can. Tell him what you need to in order to get him here, maybe invite him and his father to observe the hospital's treatment rooms."

I thought about it and then smiled. "I'll mentally ask Mom if she can show him what our resident program is."

"Now you're thinking, do it!"

After getting the clearance from mom, I called Bob. When he answered I said, "Bob this is Alice Blake calling from Kansas City. I was talking to Mother and if you're interested in a residency in Emergency Medicine at Johns Hopkins Hospital in Kansas City after graduation, she would be happy to talk to you about it. She has time tomorrow at one p.m., if that's what you want. Talk it over with your father and he's welcome to come as well, just let us know by six tonight."

"Wow! Of course I'm interested. I'll be there tomorrow with or without Dad. It just depends on his schedule. Hope to see you then. Bye."

I turned to look at Elizabeth and winked. "He's coming! His father may come too if his schedule doesn't interfere. I'll let Mom know it's on for tomorrow."

After I talked to Mom I smiled and said to Elizabeth. "I hope this works. I'm not returning from my residency for maybe three years. That's a long time."

"You're lucky. I don't know if my mother would do this for me."

"Don't kid yourself; Grandmother Jenn would walk through fire for you or my mom. Talk to her about what Barbara told us and see what she says."

At the sound of the front door closing we looked up and Grandmother Jenn was standing looking at us. "What did Barbara say?"

I said, "We asked when we could expect to meet our future husbands and she told us."

Jenn said, "Oh my! Okay, before you tell me let me sit down."

I smiled at her. "It's not that bad, at least I hope not."

Elizabeth said, "I'm supposed to meet him soon and I'll know it by a physical jolt to my body and I'm supposed to let him know I'm interested and he'll respond."

Jenn turned her head toward Barbara's picture and stuck out her tongue. "That's so like my sister. She'll give you just enough information to get you into trouble. Let me think about this for a minute. That jolt part is much like when Angel and Jeff met, but they had years to wait until they were allowed to marry. Apparently, that doesn't apply here. Okay, when you meet him… It is a him isn't it?"

"Mom! I'm not gay."

"Okay, just checking. You get the jolt and you let him know you're interested. How do you plan on doing that?"

Elizabeth looked at me questioningly?

"Don't look at me, I haven't even kissed a boy yet?"

Elizabeth's face turned crimson in embarrassment. "I'd go up to him and introduce myself, making sure I touch him in case he didn't get a jolt when I did."

Jenn said, "Not bad. But if this is going to happen soon, be sure to dress in clothing that doesn't hide your figure. I'll need to help you with your make-up too."

She turned to me. "How about you?"

"Mine's a more long term plan. It starts tomorrow when a guy I know at school is coming to the hospital to talk to Mom about a residency after he graduates next year. It was Mom's idea to get us working together."

"So there's no jolt for you two."

"Not unless it happens later when we fall in love. We're just good friends now."

Jenn said, "These long term plans are such a pain. It all depends on everything falling into place at the proper time."

I said to Elizabeth, "I told you she would walk in fire for us."

The next day I was with Mom waiting for Bob to arrive, when he and an older man were shown into her office. I stood and introduced Bob to Mother, then he introduced his father to us. Everyone shook hands and I studied Bob's father, Peter Jackson. He was a little older than Mom, stood at least six feet tall, hair was a light brown and still full, and he appeared to be physically fit. He was looking between Mom and me and thinking, *what a beautiful woman and her daughter is a younger version.*

Bob was thinking almost the same thoughts except he was projecting what I would look like in a few years. Mom said, "Let's sit and talk about your plans for the future. This hospital is now known as the premiere hospital in the mid-west because of the care we give patients and our ER department. I carry several hats here including the department head's of Emergency Medicine, Unconventional Medicine, and in a much lesser degree I supervise my niece, Elizabeth Pearson, in her healing sessions. Do you have any questions prior to a tour of my ER?"

Bob asked, "You want me to intern here for a year after graduation, and then if I'm a good fit, I'll do my residency for three or four years until you think I'm ready to take my boards. Alice is going directly into Emergency Medicine residency in Baltimore. Why there and not here?"

"Dr. Song was my mentor in Baltimore and I want her trained to take over my position here as Department Head when she passes her boards in about three years. I came from my residency to help establish this hospital, with my main interest to establish the best ER in the area. Over the years I've discovered that I must concentrate my interest in saving lives in unconventional medicine. When Alice comes back to me we'll both work separately to achieve that goal."

"So I may still be in my residency here when Alice returns."

I said, "Do you think it will be a problem working for me?"

Bob smiled at me. "Am I going to need to take Judo classes?"

"It won't be a requirement, but if you were at least a brown belt we could spar together. You look like you need some physical exercise to keep yourself in shape."

Mom said, "Why don't you show Bob the ER while I talk to Dr. Jackson for a few minutes."

* * *

After Alice and Bob left my office I smiled at Bob's father. "I should warn you that both Alice and I can read surface thoughts of others. Yours were screaming that something was going on between Bob and Alice. Actually, they are just good friends until now. Neither of them had time for romance, but there was an attraction from their first meeting. I'm just making it possible for something to happen in the future when they both are going to be ready."

"I hope he's going to be wise when that time comes. Not only is Alice a beautiful woman, but she is apparently a genius to graduate medical school in three years. I can't think of a better match for my son if it comes to pass."

"From what my daughter tells me he is a good soul. My family's path is guided by God through his messengers. That's why three of my family members have been gifted with his powers to serve mankind. If Alice and Bob fall in love and marry, then he will become part of this odyssey with us. It seems a girl from each generation receives some of God's gifts. Let's find our children and continue the tour with them."

* * *

Bob and I were in the ER talking to one of the residents when Mom and Peter Jackson joined us. I introduced the resident to Peter, explaining that Peter was a doctor from Branson and was Bob's father. The resident was Dr. Steve Collins from Harrison, Arkansas. Since they were almost neighbors, they talked for a few minutes about shared friends and acquaintances. Dr. Collins was a senior resident and would soon be sitting for his Boards.

Lilly Cox, an original RN of the hospital's ER and a personal friend of Mom's from when they attended MU together, said hello to me and then pulled Mom aside to discuss a case. Mom looked at me. "Alice, I've got a patient that needs my treatment. It's just a nasty gash that I can close without any scarring. Does Bob and Peter want to observe?"

We all wore masks, while Mom suited up in a mask, gown, and gloves before approaching the patient, a teenage girl with a jagged cut six inches long from her knee to mid-calf. The girl looked at the crowd of people behind Mom. "Who are these people?"

"They are all medical people, a doctor and students seeking knowledge. Are you ready? From past experience when I touch you there won't be any pain."

"Go ahead, they told me when you do it, there wouldn't be any scar."

Mom used her fingers to pull the skin together and worked from the top down until she finished. She used a wipe to clean the blood away and all that remained was a thin red line where the cut had been.

The girl looked at her leg and smiled at mom. "You did it, and it didn't hurt a bit."

Mom said, "Take it easy on the leg for a few days and the red line will eventually disappear. What did you do that caused the cut?"

"I was running and got too close to a fence post. Something on it cut me."

"Did anyone ask if you had a tetanus shot?"

"I couldn't remember, so they gave me one."

Mom squeezed her leg, getting her attention. "Be more careful next time. This could have been much more serious."

Mom led us to Elizabeth's healing section on the same floor. She told us that she didn't know the schedule Elizabeth had today, but she was probably still here selecting future patients. When we arrived at the Nurses Station, Mom asked for today's schedule. She then smiled at us and said, "We're in luck, she's done with her appointments for the day and we can talk to her."

We followed Mom to Elizabeth's office where she knocked on the door and we all entered at her come in reply. Mom introduced the two Jacksons, who were startled by our similar appearance to each other. Bob said, "Elizabeth, you appear a little older than Alice, but even so you look almost like twins. How is that possible?"

Mom said, "We all look like my mother and Barbara. Maybe sometime I'll show you a painting of all of us with Barbara in the background."

"Who's Barbara? I haven't heard her mentioned before."

"She's my mother's deceased sister. Elizabeth, tell the Jacksons what you're doing?"

CHAPTER EIGHTEEN

On their drive back to Branson that evening, Bob Jackson said, "Dad, what did you think of Alice and her family?"

"Son, if you fall in love with Alice and get married, that will make you the luckiest man on earth. But, you should know that they are all strong willed individuals and they have a mission in life to help others. If you get married, your duty is to help your wife fulfill that mission. Both Alice and her mother are very powerful individuals and can do things with their minds that we can only marvel at. Angel told me that she can read my surface thoughts, so Alice probably has that ability as well."

"I don't know how I can compete with a wife like that?"

"You don't try. Your job is to support her, make her job easier. She is going to be under a lot of stress when she comes back to Kansas City, taking over as the Department Head of Emergency Medicine and doing unconventional medical treatments. Hopefully by then you can help her run the ER."

"That's all assuming that we will fall in love and marry. I think I'm already past the good friend part of our relationship. I wonder if she is too."

"Son, open your eyes. Do you think all this would be happening if she wasn't."

* * *

A year later I was a resident working in the ER at Johns Hopkins Hospital in Baltimore, under Dr. Julia Song. Her lead supervisor of ER residents was Dr. Reese Hull, who seemed to delight in pushing me harder than the other residents. I had just returned from Kansas City where I served as Maid of Honor for Elizabeth's wedding to Dr. Jonah Walker, a man I had never met before. Not surprising, she met him at the hospital where he was a senior resident.

Dr. Song tapped me on the shoulder and told me to come to her office. She pointed at a chair and smiled at me. "How was the wedding?"

"Exhausting. The trip there and back and the wedding about did me in. It's a good thing I could sleep on the way back to Baltimore or I would really be dragging. Elizabeth was happy and her husband was nice, but he seemed cowered by all the close female relatives all looking alike."

"He didn't know about you looking alike?"

"Knowing and seeing isn't the same. I noticed we have two more residents."

"That's what I wanted to talk to you about. I want you to take them under your wing and show me what you can do with them."

I raised my eyebrow at her. "Did you clear that with Dr. Hull? He doesn't seem to think I can do anything right."

"That was phase one. We are now starting phase two in your training. As a supervisor you need to know how to influence your students to follow your example. Now get back to work and impress me."

I pulled my two new charges aside and told them to follow me to the break room. Once we were sitting together, I explained that I was put in charge of their training, but if Dr. Hull caught them doing something stupid it would be all our behinds. I then asked their names and backgrounds. Jack Collins was a wiry six-foot red head, with more freckles than I thought possible, who was from Boston. Lauren Higgins was a petite five-foot-three blond haired woman from Columbus, Georgia. They both had regional accents so thick that I couldn't help but smile at them.

"Do you know of my background?"

Lauren said, "You and your mother are famous for miracle

surgeries without cutting. Rumor is that you are here to earn your doctorate so that you can perform these types of treatments on your own. You hold the record for graduating from this medical school in three years and yet earned Valedictorian of your class. The previous record holder was your mother when she did the same thing in three and half years."

"Did you know I have other gifts as well? For example I can read your surface thoughts. Dr. Collins I know I look hot, but I don't appreciate you thinking of me that way, so in the future keep your thoughts on your work. I can always give you work that will purge those thoughts completely from your mind. Now follow me and hopefully we all can learn from today's experiences."

* * *

Six months later we were working injuries from a city bus crash when one of the unconscious patients awoke and broke his restraints. He easily bullied his way through the medical staff working nearby and grabbed a scalpel, threatening everyone near him. I quickly told my two charges, "Step behind me and protect your patient while I take care of this problem."

They watched goggle-eyed as I mentally snatched the scalpel from his hand into my own and then mentally restrained him as if he were in a straight jacket. Security arrived and placed him in handcuffs until I could give him an injection to calm him. I then checked for injuries among the staff and patients from his attack. No one was seriously injured and after the accident victims were treated, Dr. Song asked me and my two residents to report to her office for a debriefing.

Besides the three of us, Dr. Song, Dr. Hull and another person in a suit were present. Dr. Song said, "This is Detective Sue Love from the Baltimore Police Department who wants a report of today's problem. We can kill two birds with one report. Dr. Blake tell us what happened."

I went through the action starting with the patient breaking his restraints until he was finally subdued. My two residents then gave reports from their viewpoints. Detective Love looked frustrated as she asked, "So Dr. Blake you never physically touched the patient?"

"Not until I gave him an injection to calm him."

"You're telling me you used your mind to subdue the patient? That's just not possible. I can't put that in my report."

Frustrated, I lifted Love off the floor and then set her down again. "Is that not possible too?"

Love looked at me in surprise and a little fear. "Crap, I about wet my pants when you did that. Okay, I'll write it up as you said, but you might have to give another demonstration for anyone to believe it."

Love completed her report and had me and my residents sign it before leaving the office. Dr. Song then had us sit and contemplated her next move. "Dr. Blake you have a black belt in Judo. Why didn't you use that instead?"

"The patient was an immediate threat to all around him and I needed to use my power before my guardian angel thought I was in mortal danger. Olivia would have created a much larger problem than the use of my powers."

Dr. Song's mouth opened in surprise and comprehension. "So, the rumor of an angel protecting your mother is true."

"Yes. You can call President Smithson for a full report of that occurrence if you like. He didn't believe in angels at first ether."

"Well, let's embrace this news if it gets out. I want you to start using you're gifts in the ER as the opportunity arises. Take care of closing cuts without leaving a scar. We'll see where this takes us. Maybe Baltimore can get some of Kansas City's fame."

My two residents followed me out of Dr. Song's office like puppies after their mother. When we were back into the ER I asked them, "What did we learn from the idiot on drugs?"

Collins said, "Never take anything for granted. I thought we were safe when the patient was tied down to the gurney."

"Higgins, what did you learn?"

"That I worked for someone who knows angels and can disable a person with her mind."

"You know what I meant."

"To get behind you if things go bad!"

I smiled. "That's better, but what I was after was look at the patient for signs they were on drugs, then let me know and I'll show you what needs to be done."

I looked around the ER and it seemed slow. "Let's take a break and you can ask me questions."

CHAPTER NINETEEN

Two years have passed and the two residents under my wing are now four. The additions are two interns who selected Emergency Medicine for their residency. Taylor Chaffin is from San Jose, California, and is a five-foot-ten blond haired woman that looks like she should have been on the cover of a surfing magazine. Shelby DeLeon is from Tampa, Florida, and is a petite five-foot-two brunette whose smile would attract a male from a block away.

When I introduced the two new additions to my original residents I could mentally hear Jack Collins think he had gone to heaven. I said, "Dr. Collins, look at me."

When he jerked his head away from the new women, I said, "Remember what I said about reading your surface thoughts. You are like an open book, so hands off unless they initiate something. You new arrivals should get the skinny about me from your fellow residents. Basically, I'm going to keep you too busy for romance. Don't mess up, because then both of us will have to face Dr. Song. Whatever punishment she gives us, I will double it for you. Dr. DeLeon if you think I'm kidding about reading your surface thoughts, then consider this. That item you have in your locker that you forgot to get rid of before reporting here, better be gone before end of shift. Do you read me?"

Deleon's face turned white, then she softly said, "Yes doctor."

"Okay, let's get to work before Dr. Hull notices."

Three hours later Dr. Song walked up as I was explaining a procedure to my residents. I turned when my students were looking behind me. "Dr. Blake, when you can spare ten minutes please come to my office."

After she left I asked, "Did any of you mess up that I didn't know about?"

They all said not that they were aware of. "Okay, where was I Dr. Chaffin?"

Twenty minutes later I was knocking on Dr. Song's door. She pointed to a chair and waited until I was settled. "How do you like the new residents?"

"They are as green as grass, but eager to learn. We'll see how much they retain what I teach them."

"Speaking of grass, one of your resident's locker received a hit by one of our periodic checks by a trained drug dog, but nothing was found."

"This morning I told her to get rid of it before end of shift. I scared her when I revealed I could read her surface thoughts. I don't think we'll have any future problems with her."

Dr. Song looked at me for a moment before saying, "If you discover she or any others bring that stuff into the hospital, let me know. I'm going to post another notice about the periodic dog sniffers and blood tests for drugs."

When I returned to the ER I found my residents in the break room. I said, "Dr. DeLeon, please, follow me."

I led her into the rest room and checked to make sure we were alone, then placed an out of service sign on the door. DeLeon's face was about as white as a sheet in obvious fear. "Dr. Song said a dog sniffer got a reading on your locker. I admitted I told you to dispose of it by end of shift. My neck's on the line here because I didn't report you to her. If I ever read from your mind that you have used drugs in or out of the hospital, I'll kick you from this program so fast that you won't know what happened. They also do blood tests for drugs on a spot basis, so you still might get caught in the short term."

"You don't need to worry about that. I didn't use any of that stuff myself. A friend gave it to me to hold for him and I forgot about it."

"Friends like that you don't need, understand?"

I gave her a wet paper towel. "Wipe your eyes and compose yourself before you rejoin us. I'd put a little perfume where you had that crap to kill its smell. Don't overdo it though."

I rejoined my residents. "Bad news from home. She'll get back with us later, but don't question her about it, let her tell about it in her own way."

Three days later all the ER staff were required to take a blood test for drugs and all passed. My residents with more experience were helping me keep the others in line and DeLeon seemed to be working harder than any of them.

A month later Dr. Song called me into her office for a review of my work and that of my residents.

"Dr. Blake, continue your good work. You are at least a year ahead of the other residents. Apparently, your management style works for you in training your four residents. I've never seen such loyalty before. Dr. DeLeon seems the strongest of your four and I think it was how you handled that grass problem earlier."

"She said a boyfriend gave it to her to hold and she forgot about it. She told me she doesn't use the stuff herself."

"Well, there must have been some truth to what she said because she passed the blood test. What do you think makes your style successful?"

"Truthfully, I think they consider me a superwoman and I treat them fairly. I've never had to rip any of them more than once for the same offense."

"Okay, I'm going to move Collins and Higgins up to Dr. Hull's supervision and you get two of my slow ones. If you can't help them, I will probably drop them."

I brought my new residents together with Chaffin and DeLeon. I asked the new arrivals to give me their names and backgrounds. Amy Gentry seemed angry and dejected as she looked at me. She was about my height and physical shape even to my hair color, and was from Cleveland. Tanner Ellis was a handsome blond haired man, six-foot tall with muscles to spare, and was from Memphis. My other residents introduced themselves and I told DeLeon to start restocking medical supplies, while I told Gentry to follow me.

The break room was vacant so I told her to get a drink and I joined her at a table. She wouldn't meet my eyes and seemed to be on the verge of crying. I said, "Tell me what's bothering you?"

She jerked her head up and blurted, "You already know since you can read my mind?"

"Yes, but I need the context."

"It's that jerk you just met. He won't leave me alone and he gets both of us in trouble by the way he acts."

"Has he raped you or sexually assaulted you in any way?"

"No, so far it's just unwanted sexual advances and I can't do my job properly because of him."

"Is it just you or does he hit on all the women?"

"For some reason he fixated on me. I haven't seen him hitting on anyone else."

"Dr. Song told me to fix the problem with you two or you're both out of the program. I can talk to him about leaving you alone, transfer him to another trainer, or as a last resort remove him. What do you think I should do?"

Amy looked at me in surprise and wiped tears from her eyes. "That's the only choices? Why not supervise a meeting between the two of us so that he knows I'm not attracted to him and what he is risking for both of us?"

I smiled to myself. "Very well, I'll bring him back here and then find a better place to have that conversation."

Thirty minutes later a happier Amy and a morose Tanner had reached an understanding. He looked at Amy with respect and me with fear in his eyes after I had mentally told him what I would do to him if he failed in his promise to leave her alone. A week later the problem seemed to have resolved itself and everyone was working together as a team.

Two months later Dr. Song came by and asked DeLeon and me to come to her office. When we were seated she asked me, "Is Dr. DeLeon ready to start training a team?"

"Hey, she's the best I've got!"

"How about you, Dr. DeLeon? Do you think you can do it?"

DeLeon looked at her and then me. "Wow. I wasn't expecting this, but I don't want to leave Dr. Blake hanging. I like working with her."

I said, "Dr. DeLeon you're ready and you need the experience supervising others. Go for it."

After DeLeon left the office in search of her students, Dr.

Song smiled at me. "You did good with our two problem residents. Your team is consistently the best performing in my ER. I'm going to miss you when you leave here. You can call your mother and tell her you will be coming back at the first of the month, your time is done here as soon as you take the boards."

I smiled at her and stood to shake her hand. "Thanks for the effort you made to get me ready. I really appreciate it. Stop by and see us if you're ever in Kansas City. I know Mom would like to show off her ER."

CHAPTER TWENTY

After my arrival in Kansas City I took a cab to the hospital, arriving after the lunch hour in front of the ER. I went inside and got a wheel chair, piled my luggage on it and wheeled it into the ER until I saw a familiar face. Lilly looked at me in surprise and hurried over to embrace me and gave me a kiss on the cheek.

She asked, "You're here to stay? No more trips back to Baltimore?"

I nodded. "Lilly, you're looking really good. Anything happening"

"My oldest girl is graduating from MU and is going to medical school at Yale. How about that?"

"Julie is that old. Time really flies, doesn't it. How about your other kids?"

We talked about her family for a few minutes before I asked, "Is Mom in her office?"

Before Lilly could answer I heard a loud "Alice!" and was grabbed from behind and turned around. Dr. Bob Jackson was looking at me with a huge smile, which I returned. I pulled his head down and gave him a kiss on the lips that suddenly got seriously hot for both of us. When we broke for air we were both flushed.

Lilly looked at us in surprise. "I guess I don't have to introduce you two?"

Realizing I was on display for the entire ER, I immediately sobered up and whispered to Bob, "Get back to work; I'll talk to you later!"

Bob said, "Whoops," before hurrying away.

Lilly raised her eyebrow at me. "Whoops." Does Angel know about Dr. Whoops?"

I rolled my eyes at her and smiled. "Bob and I met as students at Johns Hopkins, but were too busy to connect except as friends. When I graduated a year ahead of him, I realized that I had a connection with him that I had been ignoring. After discussing it with Mom, she arranged an internship for him here after he graduated. We've been talking and seeing each other when we could and when I saw him just now, I let go emotionally. How many people saw us?"

"Not many. I'll talk to them later. Now get your bags and follow me. I think I know where Angel is."

We found Mom in the break room talking to one of her ER doctors, whose conversation ended just as we entered the doorway. We made room for him to leave and then I watched Mom make some notations on a clip board before looking up at me. Her face registered shock, happiness, then worry because I hadn't told her I was coming.

Lilly said, "Look who I found in the ER kissing Dr. Jackson. I'll talk to you later Alice."

Mom got up from the table and hugged me tightly and I could feel her tears dropping on my neck. She then pushed me away and looked into my eyes. "Tell me what happened!"

"I took my boards and passed, so I'm ready to begin here."

Mom's worried expression cleared for a moment. "Lilly said you were kissing Bob?"

"Our first kiss. He was greeting me and I grabbed and kissed him. From his reaction we both enjoyed it until we realized where we were. Lilly said she would talk to anyone who saw us. I hope she doesn't hang the nickname of Dr. Whoops on him, like she did after he left us."

Mom raised an eyebrow at me. "Dr. Whoops?"

"That's what Bob said after he realized where we were after we kissed."

Mom shook her head, then started giggling before breaking

out in a loud laugh, causing me to laugh so hard that we both eventually had tears running down our faces. After we were finally settled she said, "Honey, if I were you I wouldn't say that word to him ever again. I'm having a hard time trying to erase it from my memory, but I'm trying."

"Let's put your stuff in my office and go see Dr. Ellsworth. When we got to Mom's office I asked if we should first talk to dad."

Mom said, "I'm not thinking properly, you're arrival has really thrown me. There, he's now on his way here."

Mom and I were talking about my time in the Baltimore ER, when Dad arrived and gave me a big bear hug and kiss of welcome home. Mom told Dad about me passing my boards and ready to start work. He asked, "Alice, don't you want to take some time off before jumping right into the fray?"

"I'm planning on living at home, at least until Bob and I get married, so I'd just as soon be working rather than watching TV."

Dad said, "Wait a minute there! Whose this Bob you're getting married to?"

Mom said, "Jeff, she's pulling your leg. She told me they had their first kiss just a few minutes ago when she arrived."

"Oh! That's a good one, but apparently she considers him marriage material. Should we check him out?"

"Done and done, by both Alice and me. We ran a long plan on getting him here as a resident before April returned. Now April will see if the effort is going to pay off."

"With the two of you after him he's not going to have a chance."

"Oh, he has an inkling of our plans and is going along with them because he believes he's already in love with Alice. However, he is not fully aware of our family ties and what it will mean to him."

"Jeff, I'm about to take Alice to see Dr. Ellsworth and tell her of my plans for Alice and the hospital, do you want to go with us?"

"I can't. I've a surgery scheduled in half an hour. When I finish I'll get back with you and you can tell me what happened."

* * *

After I left Angel and Alice I made a fast trip to the ER in hopes of getting a look at this Bob they had plans for. Seeing Lilly, I motioned for her to come to me. Lilly said, "Dr. Blake, what can I do for you?"

"I want a look at this Dr. Bob something who Alice is interested in."

"Oh, you mean Dr. Whoops. That's him over there in booth three. He's a pretty good resident doctor. He has good hands and might make a good surgeon someday with the proper training."

"Whoops, that's an odd name. What's his nationality?"

Lilly laughed. "That's the nickname I gave him when he said that after he kissed Alice."

"Gad's Lilly, don't hang that nickname on a doctor, it will kill his career."

"Oh, you're right. Bad me, it'll never happen again. His name is Bob Jackson from Branson."

"Thanks, I better get back to work. Remember, mum's the word."

* * *

I called Dr. Ellsworth to be sure she was available and she agreed to meet with us in half an hour. To help kill time we talked about Alice's experiences supervising less experienced ER residents. "I'm surprised you didn't have some difficulty because you were so much younger than they were."

"I had a little of that, but when they heard what my abilities were they all fell in line. It really helps when you know what they are thinking, even after being told that I could read their thoughts."

"You told them that?"

"I wanted them to know if they messed up I would know and they better come to me and fess up so it could be corrected. I had the best teams of residents in the ER."

"They must have been scared of you with that hanging over their heads."

"A little at first, but then they realized if I helped them fix it, then Dr. Song wouldn't hear about it."

I looked at the time and said, "Let's head that way. I want to check on Elizabeth before we meet Dr. Ellsworth. Elizabeth was in her office selecting patients from those applying for treatment. When Elizabeth saw me she jumped up and hugged me. "You're back! Oh Alice it's good to have you back."

I held her back and looked into her eyes. "How's married life? Is he treating you right?"

Elizabeth blushed. "He's very loving and attentive. He acts as if I'm catnip to him. Angel does it ever get where he is less ardent toward me?"

"Only if you're unlucky. Jeff is still as passionate as he ever was, but I occasionally spice it up for him."

I said, "Okay, if I ever get into that position I'll know who to ask for help. Elizabeth, are you two hoping for kids or do you want to wait awhile?"

"Jonah and I have talked about it and he wants to wait until after his residency is over so that he'll have more time to be a father."

Mom asked Elizabeth, "Any problems that you need my input for?"

"No, nothing comes to mind. Here's a list of possible patients I made up for you yesterday. You and Jeff seem better suited to help them than me."

"Thanks, we better leave as we have an appointment with Dr. Ellsworth. Bye."

As we left I gave Elizabeth a little wave. "I'll see you later."

We were shown into Dr. Ellsworth's office without any wait and Janice loudly said, "Alice! You're back! She quickly came around her desk and hugged me. Let me look at you. My oh my, when you start working again people are going to have a hard time telling you two apart. Now we have three look-a-likes. It's good that Elizabeth works apart from you two. Okay Angel, what plan are you going to drop on me now?"

Mom smiled at Janice. "You know me too well. I love the ER that I started here, but I can help more people if I concentrate on my unconventional medical patients. I want to fast track Alice into taking over my duties as the department head of Emergency Medicine."

"She's a little young to head ER isn't she?"

"I started the department when I wasn't much older. Besides, she was trained by Dr. Song who cut her loose early from her residency."

Janice looked at me and smiled. "I talked to President Smithson yesterday who told me Alice had passed her boards. Alice, he's very proud of you and said you are even more outstanding than your mother, and that's saying a lot. Let's see how Alice adjusts after a month in the ER as acting head, then we'll meet again."

CHAPTER TWENTY-ONE

My first day in the ER I tried to act as if I was Mom. I wore a white wig in her hair style and wore a lab coat with her name stenciled on it. I even copied her management style. Lilly walked with me telling me the names of staff I wasn't familiar with, which worked until I met Bob. He did a double take, but I gave my head a little shake and he gave me a little smile and didn't say anything.

Several of the ER doctors asked me questions relating to their patients and I even did a no scar closing of a severe cut. After making the rounds we waited until a quiet period allowed Mom and me to make the announcement that I was the new acting head of the department. I took off the wig and her lab coat, and she handed me one with my name on it.

I said, "Staff, most of you couldn't tell the difference between Mother and me when I was working with you earlier. We are different though; however, very few changes are anticipated. Try to think of me as who you were confident in asking questions of and I won't disappoint you. If you mess up you will get burned, just as if she was here. Be warned, I'm not an easy touch, but I am fair. I'll talk to you all individually when time allows, but for now back to work. Doctor Jackson, a moment of your time."

When we were alone I asked, "I haven't checked the records of the staff yet. How long have you been a resident?"

"Two years."

"Do you want to make a career in ER or would you prefer another field?"

"I would like to try surgery to see if I have a talent for it, but if I do that it means a longer residency for me. Where do you need me the most?"

"In this hospital, doing whatever makes you happy. If you want I'll talk to Dad about getting you transferred?"

"I get two days off starting tomorrow. Let's discuss that then."

"Okay, call me and we'll get together."

The remainder of the day Mom walked me through the administrative aspect of being a department head. She gave me a nutshell background on the ER staff and I quickly learned that her ER was as good, or better, than Dr. Song's. Dr. Phillip Wasson was the lead doctor on the ER staff. He had been with the ER almost since inception and was loyal to Mom, making sure that her operating procedures were enforced.

The next day Bob and I had our discussion about his career plans. I had already spoken to Dad about the possibility of Bob continuing his residency in the surgery department. Bob said, "I would like to give myself a chance to see if I'm good enough to be a surgeon here, maybe have your dad observe a simple operation of mine and give me an opinion. Does he know about us yet?"

"Yes, but it won't make a difference if you want an honest opinion. Follow me, I've already made an appointment for you to talk to him."

When we got to his office I introduced Dad to Bob. "Dad, Bob is a two-year resident in my ER and wants to talk to you about transferring to the surgery department."

Dad said, "Lilly has already endorsed Bob as a good candidate as a surgeon, but I want to talk to him before I talk to Dr. Holmes. As department head he will need to approve the transfer."

"Alice, I know about you and Bob and we need to talk to each other without your presence coloring the discussion. So please leave and shut the door behind you."

* * *

After Alice departed, Bob and I looked at each other closely trying to judge how this relationship was going to work. I said, "So you think you have an aptitude for surgery?"

Bob replied, "I would like an opportunity to perform a minor surgery under your supervision so that you may give me an honest opinion."

"Aren't you afraid that I may be biased because of your relationship with Alice?"

"Alice says you will give me an honest opinion regardless of how you feel about me personally."

"Did you know I was in the dark about you until Alice came back? Angel and Alice had conspired to get you into this hospital so that when she returned you and she could determine if you would fall into love. Is this a surprise to you?"

"Not really. It's too late for me anyway. I'd already fallen in love with her before she returned to Baltimore to start her residency."

"That kiss she gave you when she returned was your affirmation that she felt the same way?"

"Yes. I was so surprised that I lost myself in the kiss, right there in front of everyone."

"Bob, regardless how this surgery turns out, I want to welcome you into the family. May God have pity on you for what you are about to receive. Don't get me wrong, I've enjoyed my connection with this family no matter what I've had to endure. This afternoon I'll prep with you for a minor surgery and hopefully all I'll have to do is observe."

* * *

Bob found me in the ER after leaving the meeting with Dad. He told me that he was scheduled to perform a minor surgery this afternoon with Dad observing. I asked, "Did he say anything about the family when you talked to him?"

"Well, he welcomed me to the family no matter how the surgery went. He seemed to infer that the men don't have an easy time being married to one of you, but the rewards make it worthwhile."

"I think he means we women make a special effort to keep you happy. When you transfer to surgery that's going to add another three or four years to your residency. I'm not sure I can wait that long to marry you."

"That's putting the cart before the horse isn't it? Remember, I haven't asked you yet."

"Oh poo! We both love each other, so it's only a matter of time. Are you going to wait until we are in a romantic place or is it going to be a spontaneous event?"

"I think it's going to be the latter, because you can read my mind for any plans I make, which would spoil the surprise."

"Oooh, I like that. Come with me a minute I've got something to show you."

I pulled him into a nearby storage room and gave him a passionate kiss, which led to a little groping that I eventually had to put an end to before we both lost our minds. We straightened our clothing and I checked for any lip stains on his face and collar before we left the room separately.

I went to the rest room to check myself in a mirror and reapply lipstick, before returning to duty. I thought, *I'm definitely not going to be able to wait that long for Bob to finish his surgery residency. Maybe another year and that's it. I'm going to talk to mom about this.*

That night after dinner, I met Mom in the bedroom for a little woman to woman talk. I told her about my passionate meeting with Bob today and my unwillingness to wait very long to marry him.

"Honey, I felt your spike of emotions and I understand your frustration. Your dad and I had to wait six long years before we were allowed to wed. Talk about frustration, on our wedding night we broke the bed."

"I want to marry Bob as soon as possible, but no longer than a year after he starts his surgery residency. Do you think I'm being unreasonable?"

"No. Has Bob proposed yet?"

"We talked about that today and he wants it to be a surprise, so no romantic preparations that I can read from his mind. I kind of like that and I know he's as hot for me as I'm for him."

"Cool that ardor down. You don't want hospital gossip about you two when you're his boss."

"Okay, I wonder what Dad actually said to Bob? Oh well, it didn't seem to adversely affect how he feels about me. Is it alright if I invite him over for dinner tomorrow?"

"Sure, why not. Do you know what kind of take-out he likes?"

"No, just order what you normally do. I can get his likes and dislikes as we get to know each other better."

Bob showed up for dinner and I introduced him to my mom's copy of Barbara's picture. Bob said, "She's a beautiful woman. Is she who you are all patterned from, because it's unreal how close you resemble her."

"She's my great aunt. My mother's, mother's sister. We all look alike, including my Aunt Elizabeth. Barbara was engaged to marry my grandfather, but she died shortly thereafter. Eventually he married Barbara's younger sister, Jennifer or Jenn as we call her. Barbara gave the original of this self-portrait to grandfather before she died. The original and copies have been used by the family to talk and receive messages from Barbara, who is now a messenger from God. Any questions?"

"I'm not sure I'm following all this. Barbara must be an angel to be a messenger from God, right? Do you talk to the picture and then get a response somehow?"

Bob was looking at me as if he had missed something in my exclamation when Barbara suddenly appeared before us causing Bob to step in front of me in a protective posture. I quickly stepped around him. "Barbara this disbeliever is my future husband Bob Jackson. He is a resident doctor at our hospital."

Barbara said, "Another doctor in the family. He has the right instincts, but does he know how powerful you are? Bob, do you have a question for me?"

I looked at Bob, whose mouth was hanging open, and gave him a nudge with my elbow. He shook off his paralysis. "You're her. The beautiful woman in the picture. So it's true, you're an angel. I love Alice and want to marry her. Do you have a problem with that?"

"My, Alice I think you have a keeper here. No problem here, but be aware that we watch over our daughters and you better treat them with respect and love or face the consequences. Anything else?"

"Are all the offspring of your daughters limited to daughters, or are sons allowed as well?"

"From this point forward the first offspring will be a daughter, followed later by a son if that is desired."

Angel, who had been following the conversation, asked, "Does that mean if I decided to have another child it could be a boy?"

Barbara looked at her for a moment before responding. "Angel, if that is your desire then you may have a son."

Jeff placed his arm around Angel and they mentally talked to each other about what they both desired. Angel said, "We're not certain yet what we want to do, but a son would be nice."

Barbara said, "Alice, remember that your first born will be a daughter that will eventually have all your powers. It has not been decided what powers any sons will have. Daughters handle power better than sons, so some thought will be given this question."

Barbara disappeared back into the picture and the family looked at each other in wonder at what had been revealed. Angel said, "Bob, you did good with that question. I thought it was written in stone that we would only have daughters and never asked the question about having a son. I wonder if Mother would consider having a son..., no she's much too old now. Alice, how about you? You and Elizabeth both have that option now."

I put my arm through Bob's and squeezed. "We'll talk about it when the time is right. We need to talk to Jenn and Elizabeth with this news. Do you want to do it now or wait until tomorrow?"

Mom said, "I'll mentally contact Mother and you can tell Elizabeth."

After we had both finished with our mental calls, Mom asked Bob if he had a favorite delivery food choice and handed him a variety of menus. Thirty minutes later we were eating Chinese with Grandmother and Grandfather Pearson who lived next door. They had let us know they were coming, so we had ordered enough for everyone. Grandmother Jenn was very interested in what Barbara had disclosed, because this was a big change from the past.

Angel said, "Mom, she said the son may not have the powers of the daughter. The reason given was that daughters could handle power better than sons."

I said, "That will be quite a handicap for a son, whose older sister is so powerful compared to him. Maybe, they could give him his powers a little at a time and see how he adjusts with what he has."

Bob said, "I think you're trying to over think this. Jeff, you and Jack aren't resentful because of your wife's powers, are you?"

Jeff replied, "No, but it's not the same thing. I can see resentment building over the years watching your older sister display her wealth of powers, while he had little or nothing in comparison."

I said, "You think that's the reason for only daughters until now?"

Jack said, "I think that's a valid point, but I believe if he's raised properly and the sister is not more than a year or two older, the son and daughter will establish a bond that jealousy can't break."

Angel said, "Well, we will have to wait until God's minions decide what they are going to do. Their decision will determine on whether I will seek a son."

CHAPTER TWENTY-TWO

Bob and I were in the process of getting married almost a year after he started his surgical internship. Dad said he had a gift for surgery and expected him to join the team almost as fast as his own internship. As Mom was putting the finishing touches on my gown she said, "Alice, you poor girl. You've done the same thing I did, marry an intern and not have the time for a honeymoon. But, I understand your reasoning. I was sexually frustrated too and couldn't wait any longer."

"Yeah, all we get is a long weekend, but I'll make sure we both remember it. I'm glad I talked Bob into getting a larger apartment. It was just too small for both of us and I've got room to hang Barbara's picture. Maybe you can help me move my stuff into it after Bob and I return to work."

My bridesmaids were my two roommates from Johns Hopkins University, Candy Thompson and Viola Simpson. My maid of honor was Barbara Messing-Peterson. She was as close to being family without being blood kin as she could get. She'd been Mom's maid of honor too and was getting a little old for the job, but I thought she would break down and cry when I asked her to do me the honor, so I was sure I did the right thing.

Barbara Messing-Peterson and I met my old roommates at the airport and returned to the Hyatt Regency for my pre-wedding party. While they checked in, Barbara and I went to the bar and secured a booth for us. Barbara had married Dr. Bob Peterson about five years ago after a long courtship and she said she was enjoying married life. Barbara and Elizabeth were very close as they shared painting. Elizabeth had asked Barbara for help when she first started with watercolors and it progressed from there. Elizabeth's talent grew and was now showing and selling her own works.

Candy and Viola soon joined us and we caught up on each other's careers. Candy was working with her father in Chicago and Viola was working in a hospital in Santa Fe. I explained to my old roommates that Barbara is an old family friend and was a well known painter. Viola said, "You're that Barbara Messing! I've seen your work and you're famous. You did the family portrait whose copies were used for healing associated with Alice's mother."

"Yes, that publicity helped in getting my name recognized as a painter. Jenn's other daughter is now a healer and a painter. You should check out Elizabeth Pearson-Walker's work while they are still reasonably priced."

My roommates looked at me in contemplation before Candy asked, "What's happening with you besides getting married to the guy you claimed was only a friend?"

"I'm the department head of Emergency Medicine, and along with my mother treat patients in the hospital's unconventional medicine department. If you girls want to add working at the world famous Johns Hopkins Hospital in Kansas City to your résumé, I have some influence here."

Viola said, "So that wasn't just hyperbole when you said you needed to get through medical school as quickly as you could so that you could return to Kansas City and help your mother in saving lives."

"Yes, but I didn't realize she wanted me to take over her beloved ER because she was so overworked. Now that I've done the job I realize how much time is takes and understand mother's decision."

Viola said, "I work in the ER at my hospital and wouldn't mind working with you here. Just how tough are you to work for?"

I gave her an evil smile. "Not any worse than if Julia Song headed the department."

"That bad huh. How soon can I start. I've missed the drama

after you left."

"Stay over until Monday and talk to Dr. Ellsworth, our hospital administrator. I'll let her know you're coming and put in a good word for you. I'm looking forward to seeing you when you report to duty."

The wedding was a blur to me until we kissed at the end. Then it was like a fast forward until Bob carried me over the threshold of our apartment. He set me down inside where we kissed each other passionately, then it was a race to see who could disrobe faster and run naked into the bedroom. I won because I wasn't wearing any underwear.

When Bob joined me on the bed he slowly drew me into his arms and gave me a long kiss that curled my toes. We explored each other's bodies until our passion exploded as we made love. After making love three times I got up and fixed us some food that didn't involve crackers, and brought it back to my husband, hoping to refresh him sufficiently to continue our lovemaking.

The next morning I was awakened by a soft kiss on my lips. I opened my eyes to behold a naked god bearing breakfast on a tray, which he placed in my lap after I sat up in bed. He quickly crawled into bed with me and we took turns feeding each other pieces of fruit with our fingers. When the fruit was gone he placed the tray on the floor and started to kiss and lick the juicy syrup off my face and chest, which I then reciprocated. Later, we took our first shower together, where we eventually made passionate love until the cold water chased us out. Using our new fluffy towels, we dried each other off before returning to the bed where we took turns giving each other massages.

We lay naked in each other's arms basking in our love for each other until we fell asleep. Several hours later I woke and looked at my new husband in wonder thinking, *so this is love. I almost ache when he's not in my arms, and when we make love it's as if we are one. I wonder if he feels the same as me?"*

Alice you have no idea how you complete me. Is this normal for me to mentally talk to you like this?

Yes, because I'm touching you. I didn't want to freak you out before, so I didn't think at you when we touched before. We can mentally talk to each without touching now because we have joined minds.

This is almost as intimate as making love. Does this work with others in the family?

Mom and I can read anyone's thoughts without touching. That's a gift none of the others in the family have.

I told him how to block Mom's or my mental scans, but didn't warn him that we could do it from long distance. There was no way a person could blank out their thoughts all the time. I asked Bob, "How much time do we have before you need to get ready for work?"

"Not enough time for what you have in mind, but I can snuggle a few more minutes. What are your plans for today?"

"Mother is going to help me move my things into the apartment, then we'll spend the rest of the day at the hospital. I'll check in with you when I get there. Would you bring in my change of clothes from the car, or I'll be stuck wearing my wedding dress driving you to work."

Later, after Mom and I had brought my things into the apartment and temporarily stacked them out of the way, she helped me hang my copy of Barbara's self-portrait in the living area. We both sat together on the couch looking at the picture when she asked, "Well, how did you and Bob get through your wedding night?"

"Well, I didn't kill him with sex, but he gave out after three bouts and I had to feed him to get his strength back up. Is that normal?"

"I don't know, I've only been with Jeff and his staying power increased with practice. Maybe Bob will too. Did you enjoy yourselves?"

"I certainly did and I made sure he did too. Did you ever do anything kinky?"

"Honey, what you and your husband do in bed is not my business, but Jeff and I found ways to increase our pleasures with each other by using our imaginations and with our powers we can do things others can't."

Later that day I checked in with Bob and then went by Dr. Ellsworth's office to see if Viola had seen her. Janice smiled as I entered her office. "How's the newlywed?"

I gave her a sly smile. "I think I wore him out. I just checked in on him and he looked pooped. Did Viola Simpson apply for a position?"

"Yes, and I sent her to the Human Resources Department to start the paperwork. She should be back here next week."

"Great, I'll go see if she's still in the building."

I found Viola still filling out forms when I entered the Human Resources office. She looked up as I entered the room and rushed to hug me. "I didn't expect to see you here today. Couldn't you get a day off?"

"I could, but Bob's a resident and you remember how little time they have off. Are you about done with the paperwork?"

"Almost. When I finish would you take me for a tour of your ER?"

"Sure. When is your flight home?"

"I've got four hours before its scheduled to leave."

After Viola turned in her documents and they were checked over, we headed toward the ER. I stopped and let Viola look at the room and it's activity. Lilly saw us standing there and came over. "Dr. Blake-Jackson, can I be of assistance?"

"Wow, my new name took me by surprise. Lilly, this is an old roommate from medical school, Viola Simpson. I've just hired her as a new ER doctor starting next week. Viola, this is Lilly Cox, one of our most experienced nurses. She was a roommate of mother's when they both attended MU. Her husband is also a nurse here and they are the backbone of our nursing staff."

Lilly left us and returned to her duties, while I started showing Viola around the ER. When finished I took her to the break room and asked her if she had any questions.

"Alice, it's huge. My old ER is not even half as big. The layout is somewhat similar to Baltimore's, but different too." "What shift did you work at Santa Fe?"

"New arrivals work the least desirable midnight shift. I assume that's where I'll start."

"Actually, you will have your pick. We are presently at full staff."

"Wow! You do have pull. I'd like the eight o'clock shift then."

"When staff mess up I transfer them to the midnight shift until someone else's mistake brings them back. It seems to work out well, because if they mess up on the midnight shift too, then they're gone. I have a very good core staff, manning that shift, and like being there."

"I can see why your staff tries to do their best. Do you have anyone presently on the midnight shift as punishment?"

"No, so far I've only had to do that once and he quit after a week."

"How many residents does the ER have?"

"We currently have five. Normally we have two for each of the three years expected for this position, but Bob transferred his residency from here to surgery a year ago. We'll be up to six in another month when we get two more from Baltimore."

Viola and I talked about our respective families until it was time for her to leave for the airport. She told me she would email me when she arrived back into town. I checked on Elizabeth after Viola left. She took a break when I arrived and we talked about our marriages like sisters, rather than aunt and niece. Eventually, we talked about the possibility of having a son.

We both had residents as our husbands and neither wanted to start a family until they were permanent staff. Elizabeth's husband, Jonah Walker, is scheduled to take his boards next month, while Bob has at least two more years before he would be ready.

Elizabeth said, "According to Barbara, my first child is going to be a daughter, so the son question is moot for me until after she is born. If I have a vote, I want equal powers for the son. Besides, if my line are going to be healers he should share in the responsibility."

I nodded. "I foresee problems developing if that doesn't happen. I haven't discussed this yet with Bob, but if the siblings don't have equal powers, I don't want a son."

Mom showed up shortly thereafter. "Girl's, your conversation was so loud in my head that I thought I had better calm you down. Remember, Barbara said no decision had been made yet. Let's wait until we hear what has been decided. If we don't like it, then we can try to change their minds."

Elizabeth said, "Angel, have you given any thought about having another child?"

"Some. I'm not getting any younger and my window of opportunity is not going to stay open much longer. However, I'm going to wait until the matter of the son's powers is decided."

CHAPTER TWENTY-THREE

Three years later Bob passed his boards and was now a staff surgeon. Elizabeth has a two-year-old daughter and I just learned I was pregnant. Bob was ecstatic about the news of being a father, but we haven't told anyone else yet. I was saving that announcement for a previously planned birthday party for Mother tonight in my Grandparents' condo.

At the party and after the celebration had wound down somewhat, I told Mother. "I'm pregnant!"

Mother's eyes widened in surprise, then she hugged and kissed me. "Honey, you're about six weeks into your pregnancy; did you just find out?"

"I discovered it a few days ago. I told Bob and decided to wait for this party to tell everyone else. Touch me again and verify what I'm thinking."

Mother touched my stomach and after seeing her lips tighten against her teeth I knew she saw it too. She looked at me with a concerned expression. "Alice, you're going to have twins!"

At that announcement, everyone in the room fell silent and looked at me, then as one we all looked at Barbara's painting for an explanation. Barbara cleared her throat, letting us know she was standing behind us.

I said, "Twins is new. What's the explanation?"

"It was decided to try an experiment and have the daughter

and son born together, hoping for a closer bond between them. The daughter will arrive first, closely followed by the son. They will grow into their powers as they age, starting when they are five. If this experiment succeeds, then future births will be twins, each with full powers. Angel, I know what you want. I can give you a daughter now or if you wait ten years and if the experiment is a success, then you may have twins."

Mother grimaced. "I don't want to be a mother that late in life. Jeff, do you want to raise another daughter like April?"

Dad hugged both of us in his arms and looked at me proudly. "Raising this one was a delight. I'm sure her sister will be the same."

Grandmother Jenn Pearson said, "Wow! Angel, your birthday gives us all something to celebrate. More children and the first son is on the way. Alice think of an appropriate name for our first son. Make it full of promise for the rest of the family."

I winked at Bob. "I guess we can name him Adam and his sister Eve."

After the laughter died down, Grandmother Pearson said, "That's a good first try, but just a little too suggestive."

I considered several male names and softly said, "Aaron. Aaron and April. Bob, what do you think?"

"Aaron, that's a strong name. A teacher or priest, a brother of Moses. April is which grandmother?"

Grandfather Jack Pearson said, "That's my mother's name. She died in a car accident when I was five and I was saved by Olivia."

Bob asked the others. "I think they're great names. Anybody have any problem with them?"

When Bob and I got back to our apartment, I realized that with our expected additions we needed a larger place to live. "Bob, we need to start looking for a new apartment. I've heard of some new ones not far from the hospital. Let's check them out this weekend."

The next day Mom entered my office with a concerned expression on her face. I asked, "What's wrong?"

"Dr. Ellsworth is retiring, which means we'll be getting a new hospital administrator. President Smithson retired three months ago and that doesn't leave us with anyone else that I was associated with when we opened this hospital."

"How about Dr. Jacob Holmes? He was Baltimore's lead

surgeon when he came here with Dad as his only resident. He may be tagged for Janice's job. Let's see if he might be interested."

Mom knocked on Holmes' door and we entered. Holmes looked up and seeing the two of us, said, "Well, if it isn't two of the Pearson triplets. This can't be good news, what's up?"

Mom said, "We want you to apply for Janice's position, she's retiring!"

"What! Crap, I've got some building programs in process and without her it might not happen. Have you talked to her to see if a replacement has been decided upon?"

Mom said, "No. Let's go together and maybe we can get some answers that we can act upon."

They arrived at Dr. Ellsworth's office and her receptionist smiled at them. "Go right in, she's been expecting you."

I was struck by how much better she appeared than the last time I had seen her. It was as if an enormous weight had been lifted from her shoulders. She looked at us with a slight smile on her face. "Well, which of you elder two want my job? I've got two letters of recommendation here, which should I email?"

I said, "Mom can't do it because of her other responsibilities. Dr. Holmes seems the best choice if he can tear himself away from being a surgeon. How about it Jacob, do you want to run the best hospital in the Midwest?"

Holmes looked at us as if we each had two heads. "Are you crazy, I couldn't do what Janice does. I don't have the experience."

Janice said, "I didn't either when I got the job. I learned as I grew into the job. I'm sure that the three women who put this hospital on the map will give you all the support that you need. You don't want an outsider to come in here and mess things up, do you?"

"Crap! When these two showed up in my office with the news that you were retiring I got a cold chill. When is your retirement date?"

"Three months from Monday. I can give you a crash course in what you need to know before I leave. The department heads pretty much do the heavy lifting, I just report to Baltimore and handle the PR when one of our three miracle workers does something unusually magnificent."

"Well, I don't have to worry about who replaces me as

department head. Jeff will fill that slot nicely. When Angel initially told me how good a surgeon he was going to be I had no idea he would replace me. Alice's husband, Bob, is well on his way to being as good as Jeff. You two both married world class surgeons."

Jacob looked at Janice for a moment, thinking. "Okay, send my name in. I hope I don't miss being a surgeon too much."

I said, "On a lighter note, I'm pregnant with twins, a boy and girl."

Janice looked at Mom in surprise. "Is this the first boy for your family?"

"Yes. Barbara told us it was an experiment, and future boy birth's would be determined by how well Alice's son handles his powers."

I said, "Apparently, they believe my daughter will be a stabilizing influence on him. Since this is a test, anything is possible. We'll just have to watch them closely and see what happens."

I stopped by the ER on my way back to my office where I asked Dr. Viola Simpson and Lilly Cox to join me in the break room. When we were settled at a table I broke the news about my pregnancy with twins.

Lilly said, "Twins? Your family has always had single birth girls, what's happening?"

"We wanted boys, so the angels are trying an experiment with me and I get one of each sex."

They both stared at me in awe before Viola asked, "Does this mean they will have your powers?"

"Barbara told me they will begin to get their powers when they are five years old. Actually, that will make it easier on me because I had some of my powers at birth. Mom had her hands full with me. Either of you want to volunteer to babysit my little darlings?"

Lilly smiled at me. "As long as they aren't five yet. I don't think I can handle them walking up walls."

"Surely you're joking?" Viola said doubtfully.

I said, "A little, but if they are like me they will eventually move objects with their minds, including themselves. Oh, the joy of raising gifted children."

Viola said, "George and I are getting married next month. I'm glad I don't have your problems when we start having kids. How do you cope?"

"I was born into it. It's my normal. Aunt Elizabeth's daughter, Jennifer, is two and hasn't shown any additional powers yet, so she may only be a healer like her mother. She told me that she was anxious to see how my son handles his powers, because she wants a son."

* * *

Three years later I had adjusted to raising my twins, April Miriam and Aaron. April was born before Aaron, consistent with the family's record of having daughters as first born. Our theory of what the small cross birthmark represented was proven wrong because Aaron had the same birthmark as his sister. It must just be a family connection. Elizabeth's daughter, Jennifer, recently came into her healing powers when she turned five.

We had a family meeting where we discussed with Elizabeth the proper time to introduce Jennifer to the hospital's healing program. Both Mom and Elizabeth used their own early experiences when they both started healing to reach a plan. When Jennifer is eight, she would periodically join her mother when she did her healings. After a period of time when she was judged to be ready by Elizabeth, Jennifer would gradually do healings until she was ten. At that time Elizabeth and Mom would make a determination if Jennifer was ready to work a full four hour shift.

Jennifer was currently being home schooled and was taking computer courses much like the other daughters had done, including myself. My little darlings were now walking and talking, but it seemed they didn't need to talk with each other. Barbara told me that they wouldn't come into their powers until they were five, but I suspected otherwise. I was at home alone with the twins while Bob was gone having the car serviced. I picked them both up and mentally asked them, *kids can you hear my voice?*

They both looked at me intently and grinned in delight. April answered, *mommy is that you? I thought only Aaron and I could talk this way.*

No, Grandmother Angel and I can mind talk as well. Have you been doing it long?

Aaron mentally said, *we could talk this way before we talked with our mouth. Why are you now talking to us this way?*

I was misinformed when you were able to do this. But, that's okay. Let's keep this a secret between us and Grandmother Angel. We'll surprise her the next time we see her. Can you hear the thoughts of others?"

April said, *No Momma, but I thought only we could do this until you spoke to us.*

Can you move things with your mind? I said and then demonstrated by mentally picking up a toy and have it float in front of them.

Aaron said, "Mommy, show us how to do that."

I let the toy drop. "Use your mind to feel the toy. Can either of you do that?"

April said, "I think so, now what?"

"Concentrate on the toy and visualize it rising into the air."

The toy moved slightly, then slowly started moving upwards. Aaron said, "Wow! Can I try now?"

The toy dropped to the floor and we watched Aaron's face as he concentrated on the toy until it slowly moved upwards. It was soon joined by another toy controlled by April and they started moving the toys around the room and then into their hands.

They both looked at me in anticipation of new tricks, but I thought it was rules time. "Okay you two. Now that you are beginning to come into your powers you have to follow certain rules of what is acceptable and unacceptable, do you understand me?"

Aaron said, "Yes Mommy. What we are allowed to do and what is not allowed."

"Okay. Number one rule, outsiders shouldn't see you using your powers unless I say you can. Number two, don't mentally lift people including yourselves unless I or daddy are present. There will be more rules as you gain more powers. Please let me or daddy know when you can do something new, and don't scare Mrs. Brown with what you can do. It's better if she doesn't know or we may have to get another nanny."

I mentally called Mom and asked her to stop by as the twins were coming into their powers earlier than expected. Thirty minutes later she arrived with Dad. I explained to them how I had introduced telekinesis to them after I discovered they could mentally talk to each other. When we entered their playroom the twins immediately ran to their grandparents and hugged their legs while shouting, "granma and granpa."

Mother sat in a chair and had her grandchildren sit in her lap. When they were settled she mentally said, *Aaron, April, I understand that you can mentally speak with each other and now with your mother. Is that true?*

The twins each gave her a nod while smiling eagerly. April said, *Oh, now we can talk to you too granma. How about granpa? Can he talk to us this way too?*

No, just your mom and now me. You must be careful about people other than family knowing about your abilities. Other children especially, because they can't keep a secret. Can you show me what you can do so far?

April said, "Mommy can Aaron and I show Granma and Granpa what we can do?"

At my nod their faces showed their concentration and then two toys rose from the floor and into the air where they circled each other until one landed into each grandparent's lap. Mom said, "That's pretty good, but stick with soft toys until you get really good. That way maybe you won't break anything or hit somebody in the head by mistake."

Bob walked into the room. "What's up?"

I told him of my discovery of our children's early development of their powers. He looked at their smiling faces and smiled. "Kids, it looks like you've been having fun. Just remember the rules Mom and Grandmother have told you so no one gets hurt."

Bob whispered in my ear, "You did give them rules?"

At my nod, he sighed and asked them to show him what they could do. Mom stood beside me as we watched the children perform for their father. She quietly said, "Bob is really quite quick on the uptake for the short time he has been with us. You have married well and now are the first to have twins. I wonder why they have gotten their powers early?"

I watched the twins move toys mentally. "Maybe, someone wants a faster resolution on how Aaron handles his powers."

CHAPTER TWENTY-FOUR

Three years have passed and my twins, Aaron and April, are almost six. They appear to have fully come into their powers and they have the same gifts as mother or me, although they are not yet as powerful. I expect them to gain strength as they age, much as I did.

April is the dominant personality of the two and is the first to try something new. When they started kindergarten, Aaron was protective of his sister until he was sure she could take care of herself. They were under strict instructions not to use any of their gifts unless it was to protect themselves.

Three months into kindergarten all the children were outside playing in a high board fenced playground located at the rear of the classroom. Suddenly, a car crashed through the fence heading toward the children when it suddenly stopped, as if hitting a wall. I learned later that Aaron and April acting as one mind stopped the car by using their powers. The teacher rushed the children back into the building and called 911. Apparently, the driver blacked out after having a medical emergency and was rushed to my ER.

I didn't know about the accident until after the driver had been examined and admitted to the hospital for treatment. The male driver had suffered a heart attack and was in stable condition. Later that day after we were all home, I questioned the twins on what actually occurred.

April looked at her brother. "We didn't think, but just reacted to the car heading toward us. We used a stop thought and it worked. The car stopped right there before it hit anyone. Did we do the wrong thing?"

Bob and I held out our arms to them and gave each a hug and a kiss. I said, "You did the right thing. You stopped the car before it hurt anybody and no one knows you did it. You didn't tell anyone did you?"

They both shook their heads. "No mommy."

"Good! How do you like kindergarten? Have you made any friends? Remember, you will start first grade before long and you may meet more children who you can make friends with."

"Aaron and I are friends with lots of kids. Can we have a birthday party and invite them?"

Bob said, "Our apartment is too small for a lot of kids. Would you like to have it at a Chucky Cheese instead?"

"Oh boy! I heard about that place. It would be great. How about it, April?" Aaron said with excitement."

April's face lit up in excitement. "Great! That's the best place ever."

I said, "Okay, your birthday's the Tuesday after next. Let's do it this Saturday at one p.m. Is that enough time for you to invite the kids you want to come?"

April said, "Yes, can you help us with the invitations?"

"Sure, it's easy on the computer. Let me help you get started."

The afternoon of the party soon arrived and the twins were on hand to greet their friends. Bob went to the reservation desk to find where our group was assigned a table. Luckily, several of the mothers volunteered to help watch over the children. There were sixteen children in our group and we were provided red stickers to put on their clothing to make it easier to track them. After everyone was seated we ordered pizzas and soft drinks for them before they scattered to play video games.

I was walking around where the children were playing keeping an eye on them, when April mentally contacted me in obvious stress, *Mommy, somebody just grabbed Nancy and is heading outside!*

Can you place a stop on their movement?

I'm afraid of hurting Nancy!

Can you freeze the door shut so it doesn't open?

Yes, he can't get it open.

Which door is it?

The back door on the east side. He's heading my way now, what should I do?

Trip him, slow him down until I get there.

Less than half a minute later I found April and Aaron facing a large man holding a young girl around her waist. The man seemed to be trying to move forward, but without success. When he saw me he dropped the girl and turned to run, but my mental stop move left him hanging in a stop action position. I started to help the girl, but my twins were already helping her up and trying to calm her distress. When she saw me she ran into my arms crying in relief.

I said, "Aaron, find Daddy and tell him to bring security back here. April, is Nancy's mother here?"

"No mommy, but I know what her cell number is."

I pulled out my cell and had her give me the number and then when she answered, I gave her a quick recap on what had happened to her daughter. She told me that she would be there in about twenty minutes, depending on traffic.

Bob arrived with a security officer, who was surprised at the prisoner's frozen position. I explained who I was and my mental powers, and the man's attempted kidnapping of Nancy. The security officer handcuffed the man and I released him from my control. He started to run again, but stopped and cowered away when my twins moved in front of him. We waited there until the police arrived and took our statements before we rejoined the birthday party. By this time Nancy's mother had arrived and at her daughter's insistence they joined the party as well.

Aaron and April had Nancy sit with them while they cut the birthday cake and then helped hand out the portions to her classmates. Before we left the building after the party, Nancy and her mother Julia Mason thanked Aaron, April, and me for keeping Nancy safe. Nancy gave the twins a hug and kissed me on the cheek before leaving.

The Sunday's edition of the *Kansas City Star* had a picture of me and the twins with Nancy, along with a column about how we had saved Nancy from being kidnapped. Later that day I got a call from Dr. Holmes. "Congratulations to you and the kids on saving the little girl, but you know this is not going to be the end of it. Odds are when the news service picks up on this, you're going to go national."

"I know. I've been trying to keep this low key for the sake of the kids. Maybe we'll luck out."

"Maybe you should caution your kids not to talk to anyone about the kidnapping without you or Bob being present."

"You might have a good idea there. I'll talk it over with Bob before we do anything. Have you heard anything from Johns Hopkins' new President, Walter Henson? The previous one didn't last very long."

"Henson is a graduate of Johns Hopkins, so he may have better luck in understanding the scope of the organization. He's called a meeting of all the administrators of the various schools and hospitals in two weeks, so maybe we will learn if there's going to be any changes."

After ending the call with Dr. Holmes I told Bob what was discussed. He thought about it for a few moments before saying, "Let's have that discussion with the twins, but one of us should take them to school and discuss with the principal about their policy about allowing the press on school grounds."

I mentally called the twins to come to us for a family meeting. They both soon arrived and April asked, "Did we do anything wrong?"

"No, in fact you both have done everything a parent wishes their children would do. April, you did something some adults would be fearful of doing. You followed the kidnapper of a friend and asked for help from a parent. Aaron, you responded to this mental plea from your sister and joined her in her efforts to restrain the kidnapper until help arrived." Bob said and then held out his arms toward his children, who responded to his hug with smiles.

I said, "This heroic act on your part has brought the attention of the news media. I'm going to try to shoulder the use of the psi powers used in the kidnapper's capture. I'm going to say I saw April motion for me to follow her to the back room where I subdued the man by the use of my powers. Do you know of anything other than the kidnapper's testimony that would counter this statement?"

The twins looked at each other as they mentally conversed

with each other, then April said, "No, Nancy didn't understand what was going on except that the kidnapper had grabbed her and was trying to get out of the building with her. She knew we were there, but not what we were doing. Aaron and I haven't said anything about what we did. You don't want our powers known to others because it may adversely affect our relationship with the other students?"

"Yes, if it does then you'll have to be home schooled and you will miss out on the social relationships provided by your interactions with the other students."

Aaron said, "You and Grandma Angel were both home schooled. Is this why you want us to attend school so badly?"

"Yes, we both missed out on interactions with other people until we attended college. It's hard to make adjustments without those early interactions. However, we did it and you can too if this doesn't work out as I plan. Any other comments or questions? …Well, until I tell you otherwise, don't talk to anyone about the kidnapping unless one of us is present and we give you our permission."

The next morning I took the kids to school and they showed me were the principal's office was located. I had the kids sit outside while I talked to Principal Paula Crowder. Apparently she had read the *Star* article about the kidnapping, as she rose and greeted me by name. I quickly filled her in on my concerns with media coverage involving my children and asked that my children not be questioned about their part in Nancy's rescue.

Crowder said, "Only approved visitors are allowed on school grounds and that does not include the news media. If they arrive I'll let you know so that you may arrange for your children's safe pickup from the school. Would you allow them to be acknowledged for their bravery by a school assembly?"

"Yes, but just use the information contained in the news article when you describe their actions. I'd like them to fit into the school with the least amount of disruption."

Before I left the school I mentally told my twins, *you can repeat the cover story we agreed upon and the school plans to honor you before the other students. Have fun and don't be nervous.*

I gave them both a hug and kiss and they watched me leave

with a little misgiving about the prospect of standing before the whole school.

* * *

April mentally said, *it's okay Aaron. Just remember to stick with the story, if someone asks. Don't worry about the standing before all the students, I'll be right beside you. Let's find Nancy and see if she's okay.*

They soon found Nancy, who had a crowd of classmates around her asking questions. When Nancy saw us, she immediately went to April and hugged her, then blushed as she gave Aaron a tentative hug. "Class, these are my hero's. Their mother saved me, but these two delayed the bad man until help arrived."

Their teacher arrived and everyone reluctantly went to their desks. Mrs. Sizemore said, "There's going to be a special awards program honoring the Jackson twins in one hour. In the meantime, maybe we can get Nancy and the twins to tell the story of Nancy's rescue."

* * *

I arrived at the hospital to find several news satellite trucks parked near the hospital entrance. I parked in my designated space and was immediately mobbed by reporters when I got out of my car. I held up my hand for quiet. "There will be a news briefing in the media conference room in one hour. I have nothing to say until then." I excused myself and hurried away before they could recover.

My first stop was Dr. Jacob Holmes' office. Since he was the hospital's administrator, he needed to be notified of the news conference I had just arranged. When I entered his office he said, "I told you so."

"I told the media that I was going to hold a news conference in one hour. I hope the media conference room is available."

"It is. I checked when I first got here this morning." Jacob seemed to be enjoying my discomfort.

"Don't smile at me like that, it's not funny. This is going to throw off my schedule for the whole day. Let me think, maybe

Mother can help me with two or three of my appointments this morning."

"I already called her and she should be here shortly. Maybe Jeff can help you?"

"Dad's good, but not for what I have scheduled. Only Mom can fill in for that."

I looked at Jacob and smiled. "Mom's here!" Just as she walked into the room.

Jacob greeted her. "Good morning Angel. Your daughter seems to have a scheduling problem."

"I know. I saw the satellite trucks as I arrived. Alice, when's your first appointment?"

"Ten o'clock, and another at eleven. The one at one p.m. I can make if nothing else comes up."

"I can do the first one, but the one at eleven is impossible. You will have to delay it until after the news conference."

"Crap! Okay, maybe I can do that. If not I'll delay it until five p.m. The first one is the liver cancer patient I told you about."

Mom said, "How are the kids handling the publicity?"

"Surprisingly well. April is the strong one, but Aaron is doing great too. I gave them a story that shows me as the only one using our powers. If it holds up they can stay at school for a while longer. They are better at hiding their powers than I was at that age."

Jacob said, "Your twins have come into their powers? Wow, I bet you have your hands full."

I said, "They're smart and good kids who are anxious to please their parents. If it wasn't for that I would be in big trouble. They realize that God has a plan for them and with their Aunt Barbara watching over them, they are constantly reminded of that fact."

CHAPTER TWENTY-FIVE

The news conference started with me giving a background of the reason for the gathering of children. I explained April's observation of the attempted kidnapping and letting me know so that I could take action. Aaron also helped his sister try to delay the kidnapper while I hurried to rescue Nancy Mason.

When I asked for questions, a lead XYZ TV news reporter asked, "How did you stop the kidnapper by yourself? He's a very large man who's well over two hundred pounds."

"I have the mental ability to lift large weights and hurdle tall buildings." I said with a slight smile. "Do you want me to demonstrate?"

"No think you. I remember another reporter you lifted into the air."

"Darn. Are you sure? It's really quite impressive."

Another reporter held up his hand. "I volunteer. I didn't get to see the other demonstration."

I told him to come up to the raised podium so that everyone could have a better view. He was a young man in his early twenties and he quickly stepped up to the podium where I froze his body in mid-air. "That's the position security found the kidnapper, with one foot in the air and unable to move. Feel free to step closer and take pictures. Our reporter friend is in no pain, he just can't move or talk."

After several minutes of picture taking I released the young man, who almost fell before catching his balance. I asked, "Do you feel okay? Any ill effects?"

He replied that he felt fine and returned to his seat. I asked, "Any more questions?"

A reporter asked, "Did Nancy and your twins observe you using your powers?"

I replied, "Yes, that's all in the police report and no one was harmed during the event, not even the kidnapper. I've received a call from April at her school and she said Nancy was there and appeared to be fine, so my children and Nancy appear to have survived the experience without any lasting ill effects."

The questions turned to the unconventional medicine that my mother and I practiced at this hospital. I explained that we only performed treatments that was not possible under conventional methods, many that had already been told that there was nothing further that could be done for them. We generally perform four to six procedures daily between the two of us and all have been successful. My Aunt Elizabeth performs six to eight healing treatments daily, some are able to leave the hospital immediately; however, generally they spend at least two days here regaining their strength before leaving. The costs of almost fifty percent of the patients accepted are paid by the Elizabeth Foundation, which is funded by donations from the public."

I then gave them the Foundation's web page and the place where donations could be sent. Dr. Holmes took my place at the podium. "We have handouts available with all the information Dr. Blake-Jackson has discussed. If any want to take a short walk through the hospital's unconventional medicine department, please follow us and ask questions along the way."

After the walk through I made a quick stop to check on my ER. I found the department functioning well in my absence, and then checked on my eleven o'clock appointment's status. He was still willing to start his procedure that was now forty minutes behind schedule, so we would begin as soon as everything was in place.

By the time my shift was over I was back on schedule. That night during dinner, Bob and I asked the twins how school went and did they have any problems? They looked at each other and smiled, then Aaron said, "They had a special school assembly for Nancy and us where they honored April and me for helping save Nancy. They then used our story as an example for everyone to watch out for others and to seek adult help when they see something wrong happening."

I said, "Did you get nervous standing before everyone while they talked about you?"

Aaron shrugged his shoulders before replying, "I thought I was going to croak until April thought to me that I should think all those people as being only one friendly person, and it worked. I even smiled when the principal called on me to tell what I did."

Bob said, "What about you April?"

Aaron snorted. "Oh, she's not a bit shy. Since she was the one who initially saw what was happening to Nancy, she got most of the questions. April is really quick and was able to keep our story logical."

April said, "Aaron did his part well too. No one suspected we had any powers. It was all you Mommy."

I looked at my children with pride. "Kid's, I'm so lucky to have such smart children and I'm very proud of you. Do you want a special treat or something I can do for you?"

"They both ran into my arms and gave me a tight hug and kiss. In my mind I could hear them both say, *Mommy, you are the best ever. Just keep being you.*

I looked over their heads at Bob with tears running down my cheeks. He winked at me, then said, "We've raised some pretty awesome kids."

* * *

Ten years have passed and the twins are now sixteen. The family has just arrived home after attending their graduation from MU of Kansas City, both with honors. They are scheduled to start classes this fall at Johns Hopkins University, which will be the third generation from the family seeking their medical education from this institution. Angel and I were not certain that the university could handle two like us at the same time. The twins have been working with Mom and me in treating patients in our unconventional medicine department for over three years. Their minds have soaked up medical knowledge from their exposure working with us and should do well when they begin their classes.

* * *

Aaron and I stood before the picture of Aunt Barbara. I have always felt a strong attraction toward her even though I've never talked to her directly before as many of the family has. I've talked Aaron into seeking her advice before we leave home for Baltimore in a few months. While our parents were distracted with other family members I thought this was our opportunity.

"Aunt Barbara, we are getting ready to leave home soon for the first time. Do you have any advice you can give us?"

Aunt Barbara appeared before us and smiled. "If you are seeking romantic advice, neither of you are old enough for that yet. Besides you won't have time for a relationship."

"No, I know that from Mom's and Grandmother Angel's experiences. Both of us will be bringing baggage from their prior attendance at the university. How do you think we should handle this?"

"You two are better off than they were when you start. They were alone and had to cope without any help. You have each other and can solve most of your problems together. When you enroll try to have the same advisor. They may grant this since the family is known to them. Don't act superior toward your classmates, offer help if they seek it, and try to be a joiner for social events. There is no need to load up on classes, so enjoy yourselves as much as your available time allows. You both will probably be asked to consult at the hospital, do it and ask your mother what your restrictions are."

Aunt Barbara disappeared as quickly as she had arrived. I looked at Aaron and asked, "Well, that was helpful. We need to quiz Mom on dorm rooms and other living conditions at the university. Do you have anything you want answers for?"

"Yeah, but not from you or Mom. I'll ask Dad later."

I punched him on the arm, causing a frown and then a bewildered expression. "Hey, what was that for?"

"Just on general principles. You better not be planning on having a harem of women follow you around the campus."

Aaron's face flushed in embarrassment. "Where did you get that from wanting to ask Dad a question. From what I've been able to discern he was never like that."

"I'm just projecting what I know of your dating habits. You've left several of my friends with broken hearts. If I'm wrong I apologize."

"April, I've never dated the same girl more than twice and I'm still a virgin, so someone is pulling your leg. Look into my mind and verify what I just said."

I looked into his eyes and knew he was telling the truth. Aaron was never able to lie to me. "Okay, Jessie was the one spreading the lies. Why would she do that?"

"I dated her once and discovered I wanted nothing further to do with her after she embarrassed me by grabbing my crotch while we were with other friends. She appears to be after revenge when I didn't call her back."

I put my hand on his arm. "Aaron I'm sorry. I guess it's good that we are leaving her and her friends behind when we leave for university."

* * *

Six months later they were half way through their first year at Johns Hopkins University. Mom apparently greased the wheels for us because the administration was waiting for us with expectation and offered us free dorm rooms and cash as a trade for consultations at the hospital. Aaron and I each had two roommates at Wolman Hall, which is a freshman dormitory. Aaron decided to host a party where we could get acquainted.

My roommates and I knocked on his door and were greeted by a handsome guy who introduced himself as Daniel Pitts from St. Louis, Missouri. I introduced myself and my roommates, Janet Allison from Plattsmouth, Nebraska and Phyllis Smart from Clarksville, Kentucky. Aaron and his other roommate, Wesley Johnson from Petoskey, Michigan quickly introduced themselves and we mingled getting to know each other.

Within an hour we all paired up, Aaron with Janet and me with Daniel. Maybe it was because we grew up near each other, or it was because we were physically attracted to them. I mentally touched Daniel's thoughts and found he thought I was hot as well. Aaron's thoughts were confusing, but he definitely was attracted to Janet and she to him.

I gave Aaron a warning, *Cool it. This is only our first meeting. I'm attracted to Daniel as well, but we need to take this slow.*

Aaron looked at me and winked, acknowledging my message. Most of the group were drinking beer, but after the first can I switched to a coke. I wanted to keep control of my wits, even if Aaron didn't. We eventually settled together on the floor talking about our classes and worst teachers.

Daniel asked me, "I heard a rumor that your mother and grandmother both went to school here and caused a big stir about something. What's the story?"

Aaron, should I tell him the whole story or a condensed version?

Let's go with the latter for now. We can always do the full story later.

"They are both geniuses with eidetic memories and graduated as Valedictorians of their classes in less than four years."

"What! Does that mean you two are that smart as well?"

"We're pretty smart and we have eidetic memories, so if you need any help with a class we've taken we can help. Although Aaron is better in some subjects than me."

"Yeah sure. If that's true it's not by much. April is the more aggressive of us."

Janet said, "For fraternal twins you look nothing alike except for your eyes and hair color. April, who do you take after?"

Aaron smothered a laugh. "Let me show you something."

He got his laptop and pulled up past Valedictorians and showed them the pictures of Mom and Grandmother.

Janet gasped. "They look exactly alike, all three of you! That's really uncanny."

Aaron pointed at the picture on the wall of Aunt Barbara. "They all resemble her."

The group all rose to take a closer look at the picture and then compared it to April. Janet said, "It's true, except you look a little younger. That's a little strange for this to happen for three generations. Is there a story here?"

I laughed. "Yeah, but it's too long and involved for tonight.

I've got to get back to my studies and my beauty sleep. Girl's you can stay, but I've got to go."

My roomies also said their goodbyes and we all returned to our dorm room.

Once inside, Janet immediately went to my copy of Aunt Barbara's picture. "April, give me something or I won't be able to sleep tonight."

"Okay, but you'll think I'm only going to tease you. This is my Aunt Barbara, sister to my Great Grandmother Pearson. It's a photo of a self-portrait given to my Great Grandfather Pearson upon his betrothal to her shortly before her death in a car accident. He married Jennifer Powers, a younger sister of Barbara, almost nine years later. They looked similar as well. More to come if you're still interested."

"What! That's all I get?

"I told you that you would think it was a tease. Tomorrow I'll give you more. I've got to get to my studies now."

"April, you are such a tease! Okay, but you better give me more tomorrow."

CHAPTER TWENTY-SIX

Two weeks later Aaron and I received emails for us to meet Dr. Meeks at Room 226 in the hospital during our lunch break. We mentally communicated with each other to meet for an early lunch before keeping our appointment at the hospital. During the walk to the hospital we were still debating what the purpose of the meeting was about.

We met Dr. Meeks, a middle-aged woman of about my height, but about twenty pounds heavier. She introduced herself as Dr. Debra Meeks, who was assigned by the hospital to act as our liaison with the hospital for our consultations. She asked, "I need to know what capabilities you have to better determine where we may use your talents."

I said, "Are you aware of the abilities of Dr. Angel Pearson-Blake and Dr. Alice Blake-Jackson at the Johns Hopkins Hospital in Kansas City?"

"Yes, everyone here has heard of their abilities. Are you saying that you can do what Dr. Alice Blake-Jackson did when she started here?"

"Yes, maybe more since we've had several years training under them. When you start handing out assignments please alternate between us unless we are both needed for the consult."

"My, this is going to be interesting. I assume you need your doctorate in order to perform your procedures in Kansas City, just like your mother when she came here."

Aaron responded. "That's right. However, this time we aren't in a hurry to finish, so we want to enjoy our stay here."

We have an interesting case now. Would you like to give us your input since you both are already here?"

I mentally checked with Aaron and he agreed. "Sure, we'll take a look. What's the background?"

As we were walking to the patient's room Dr. Meeks told us of the child's medical history. She is twelve years old and had developed a rash on her legs that had gotten progressively worse over the week she had been admitted, and now was open weeping sores that were advancing toward her torso. Meeks stopped at a supply room and gave us a lab coat to wear, which gave us an official appearance.

When we entered the room the girl looked at us with hope in her eyes. Meeks told her that we were consultants and we each touched her body searching for the cause of her aliment. I looked up at Dr. Meeks and indicated we wished to leave the room. We walked down the hall until I was sure we wouldn't be overheard. "What has been her treatment?"

"Everything associated with rashes and nothing has worked."

"We estimate that she has less than forty-eight hours before she expires from a flesh eating parasite. As far as I know only one person has survived with the treatments currently used and there is no time for that in this case. I recommend that you use a small amount of my blood, which hopefully will cure her."

Dr. Meeks looked at me in surprise, then swallowed whatever response she started to make. "I've researched your mother and grandmother's past consults and they each volunteered some of their blood for a hopeless case. You think this is her only hope?"

"Yes, a syringe should be sufficient and I would like to see it administered. We are under strict orders when we use our blood."

We went to the nurse's station and had her obtain a syringe and draw my blood. We followed the nurse back to the patient's room and I watched as the nurse injected my blood into the IV tube. I leaned down and asked the girl, "What's your name?"

"Sally Potts. Are you going to make me better?"

"I think so. Later, when you are feeling better I will come back and talk with you. My name is April Jackson and that is my brother Aaron."

After we left the room I said, "Dr. Meeks, please let me know when she is recovered sufficiently for me to get background information from her. After she is released, please forward a copy of her medical records to Dr. Angel Pearson-Blake in Kansas City. She is keeping records of all those whom we have given blood."

When Aaron and I were walking back to the dorm he said, *I envy your confidence to make that decision without any consultation with Mom.*

Remember, Mom told us this was going to be our decision when we give our blood. We give it only as a last resort and sparingly. She and Grandmother have only done it three times in total. I guess if the occasion arises again I may have to do real soul searching before I make that decision.

Aaron hugged me, then said, "I forgot, I'm supposed to meet Janet at the library in fifteen minutes. I'll talk to you later."

I shook my head as I watched him hurry off. *I swear, for someone with an eidetic memory he amazes me on how much he forgets. Maybe it's because I blew his mind by giving blood to save that girl. Oh well, I've got some studying to do before my next class. I wonder if Daniel is free afterward.*

Two weeks later, Janet knocked on my room door lightly. I asked her inside. "What's wrong, you look awful?"

"I had a fight with your brother and I've been crying for the last hour. It's crazy because all I want is to know more about him and his family. I think I'm in love with him and I know he likes me. Why is he so reluctant to share with me?"

"Are you lovers?"

"No, and he refuses to go further than heavy petting. You both are virgins, aren't you?"

"Janet, you know from what I've told you that we are a religious family. We have contact with God through his angels and follow their instructions. Do you think we would do anything that would incur His wrath? You need to have a meeting with him and ask him to tell our full family history. Tell him that you need to have this information if you are going to be his mate sometime in the future. Tell him I said it's okay and if he prefers we can do it together when I tell Daniel."

"You love Daniel? I knew you liked him, but not to that

extent. Okay, that may be the only way Aaron will break his silence. When would you want to do this?"

"Phyllis has a date tomorrow night and is leaving at six. Let's meet here at 6:30. Wait while I check with Aaron."

Janet's eyes got big and her face turned white as she realized that I was in mental contact with Aaron. "He said the time is okay for him and Daniel, so we're on for tomorrow evening."

"You and Aaron can do telepathy!! I'm beginning to understand why you've been so secretive about yourselves."

Janet took a deep breath and calmed herself. Taking another deep breath and slowly letting it out, she looked at me in consideration. "You can read my thoughts too?"

"Only your surface thoughts. To do more would take more effort on my part and you would probably be aware that I was doing it."

"Oh, Aaron knows my most secret thoughts about him. I'm so embarrassed I don't know if I can look him in the eyes."

"We're used to it. Remember he didn't take advantage of you and I know he loves you. Think of it as a form of foreplay."

Janet blushed. "You must think I'm shameless. I've never had this attraction and passion for anyone else."

"Tell me, when we first meet our potential mates there is usually something that happens between us, did it occur when you met Aaron?"

"Not at first, but when we first touched it was like a little punch in the stomach. How about you?"

"Similar. In my case it was more a mental reaction. He seemed to glow and I had a small orgasm. My first by the way, so yes, I had a reaction."

"How in the world do you keep from physically attacking him when you're alone?"

"I've been gifted with great restraint. I just hope I don't kill him with love on our honeymoon."

For some reason Janet thought this was funny and started laughing so hard she shed tears. I brought her into a hug. Phyllis came into the room and asked, "What's happening?"

I said, "Janet is a little overwhelmed. She and my brother had a fight and just made up over the phone."

"Oh! I wish I had a serious boyfriend to get emotional about."

Phyllis had just left on her date and Janet and I were busy straightening up the common room preparing for our boyfriends' arrival. We were both nervous about this meeting, Janet on learning our secrets and me on the reaction Daniel may have on hearing it. I finally sat down on the couch and looked at the picture of Aunt Barbara. I finally had a thought and stuck my tongue out at her picture. Janet sat down next to me and took my hand for comfort. "Why did you do that?"

"Aunt Barbara has seen four generations of us going through this over the years. By this time it must be so repetitive for her. However, this time it's a little different for her. Now she has two of us to watch over."

"Your Aunt is an angel? That is so cool."

"Yes it is. However, there is a downside. How would you like someone looking over your shoulder your entire life?"

"I guess I would make sure I didn't screw up."

"Exactly. It gets tiring after awhile. I once caught myself starting to do something minor that I knew wasn't right. I didn't do it because I knew I would regret it later."

There was a knock on the door and Janet quickly opened it for the men. I had Daniel and Janet sit together on the couch while Aaron and I told our family history. The story took almost an hour with side stories for their clarifications. Janet looked at me intensively.

"April, you say Aaron is a test case for men born into the family. Assuming he passes, then women will bear twins in the future?"

"We don't know at this time, but if I was to guess it would be a yes. Aaron and I have done quite well together and I think they will stick to a winning combination."

Janet winked at Aaron. "He certainly is to me."

Daniel got up from the couch and drew me into a lingering kiss. "I like the fact that all the women in the family look alike. How do the men tell you apart?"

"Well for one thing I'm younger, and if that doesn't work they will let you know."

Aaron said, "When you see Great Grandmother Jenn, you'll see they don't age like other women. She still looks amazing like her sister Barbara, there in the picture."

Barbara was suddenly there with them. "Did somebody mention my name?"

Janet and Daniel both grabbed one of us for support. I said, "Aunt Barbara you should let us prepare them for you. You scare the crap right out of them when you do that."

"I know. That's about the only thing I get to do for fun anymore, and it only works once."

Daniel said, "Wow, you have an angel with a sense of humor. I didn't realize that she speaks directly to you and you really look like her when she's out of the picture. Barbara I don't want to piss you off, but you're really a beautiful angel."

"April, this one may give you problems after you're married. Janet, to ease your mind Aaron has passed his test and there will be future boy births for those who wish it, but only as twins with a sister. Those women not wishing twins will give birth to a girl. New comer's, if you decide to mate with these members of the family, your life will change and you will never have a boring day in your life. Any questions?"

Daniel said, "Do we have to wait until after residency before we marry?"

"No, but can you imagine these two waiting for you and not be distracted from your studies and later while working long hours in residency. You would do better if your concentration was not on them but on what you need to do to get your doctorate."

Barbara disappeared back into the picture, while Daniel and Janet appeared a little dazed by what they had experienced. I said, "Okay, I know that was a lot to digest. Why don't you men go back to your apartment and Aaron will answer Daniel's questions and I'll handle Janet's."

Daniel kissed me before turning to Aaron who was giving Janet a long passionate kiss. Janet touched her lips as she watched the men leave. "That's so crappy! I wanted more from Aaron."

"I did too. Grandmother Angel waited almost seven years before she was allowed to wed. She told me that on her wedding night they broke the bed."

Janet looked at me for a moment, then started to laugh. "That's a good one. I believed you for a moment."

"No joke. They were both so sexually frustrated they actually broke the bed."

"Crap, I don't want that to happen to us. Why not get married and live apart, except for conjugal visits. That way we would get that sexual itch satisfied and be able to concentrate on our studies."

"Mom tells me that didn't happen with her and Dad. They make love every night and would do it more except for work."

"It must be because of your relationship with God. My parents are lucky if they get together once a week. Do you think heavy petting can get us through until we get married?"

"Those before me used abstinence rather than tempt themselves with petting and they survived the experience, although it left them with a hunger for each other that is never quite satisfied. Let's talk about this some more and see if we can do it better with the least amount of problems."

* * *

We had a double wedding at the end of our first year of residency. Janet and I had talked it over and decided that enough is enough and we wanted our men. The wedding took place in my family's church in Kansas City, which was not far from any of our mate's families. Daniel's parents drove from St. Louis, and Janet's came down from Plattsmouth, Nebraska. Our parents had gotten together several times in the past since learning of our wedding plans almost six years ago.

After the wedding Janet and I were standing together in the reception line for the wedding guests when she whispered, "How much longer before we can leave?"

"Not long. After we cut the cake, we change clothes and get out of here."

"My panties are wet and my knees are knocking together so hard I don't think I can walk in a straight line."

"Me too. Let's try real hard not to kill our husbands tonight. Try to restrain yourself if he gives out after three times. Mom says to feed him if that happens."

"My mother didn't give me any advice except to bear it without crying. What's with my mother, doesn't she know making love is supposed to be pleasurable?".

EPILOGUE

280 years have passed and many changes have occurred. The original Angel Pearson line has continued to grow and expand. Kansas City is now the center of the Healing Guild, which has centers throughout the world. The guild is made up of those who heal by touch, who dress in red, and those who perform medical and other functions with their minds. These practitioners dress in blue.

The Healers are women and both groups all have a cross birthmark. The Healers represent twenty percent of the total guild members and when the general populace encounters a red-clothed healer away from the Healing Guild Center, they always give her great respect and deference. Normally there is no intermarriage between the Reds and the Blues, but if a request for marriage occurs, it requires the approval of the head of the center where they are assigned. A genetic test must reveal a direct link between them and the original founders, Jackson and Jennifer Pearson.

The offspring from an approved marriage usually become the head of a center as they exhibit all the powers of both groups.

ABOUT THE AUTHOR

Hugh A. Flowers retired after almost thirty years with the Federal Deposit Insurance Corporation as a bank examiner. He now spends his time reading and writing novels and short stories and traveling the world.

OTHER PUBLICATIONS BY FLOWERS

The SALVATION TRILOGY is a feel good story about people who are born into a destiny of God's making. They are guided throughout their lives by angels giving them instructions that sometimes are unclear as to their purpose, but reveal themselves as time progresses. Salvation is the first book in the trilogy; Angel's Triumph is the second.

Oklahoma Tomboy, Fountainhead, and Project Inception are also books written by Hugh.

www.ingramcontent.com/pod-product-compliance
Lightning Source LLC
Chambersburg PA
CBHW061234170626
46809CB00007B/2666

FINDERS WEEPERS, LOSERS KEEPERS

A NOVEL OF SPECULATIVE FICTION

MIKE MITCHELL

This work is completely fictional, but the premise is not science fiction. Who can say whether the experience described in this book has ever happened to someone in the existence we call real life. Memory and experience, time and space, are often at odds with each other, or are of compatible substances we do not fully understand. At times they seem to work in tandem to create unexpected and sometimes unexplainable events. We could say they are two sides of the same coin. This novel explores what would happen if in a toss, the coin landed on its edge. Additionally, this novel suggests there is a fifth fundamental force that works in concert with gravitational, electromagnetic, strong, and weak nuclear forces. You be the judge.

Byblos Press
Newark, Delaware

ISBN13 978-0-9990111-2-6

Published in the United States of America
First Edition

By
Mike Mitchell

Cover design and layout by Kent Bingham
More by this author check out *www.mike-mitchell.com*

BYBLOS
p r e s s